THE TURNED GODS SERIES
CHARACTER COMPANION

ALEX'S CLAIM

JOYCE
SERRANO

INTRODUCTION

Alex's story takes place approximately three centuries after *Gateway to The Nothing*, book three in The Turned Gods Series timeline.

CHAPTER ONE

Alex laid in bed, staring out the window at the dull gray sky. The sound of tiny raindrops rhythmically tapping against the windowpane made him want to roll over and cover his head. He had forgotten rain had been scheduled for today. How unfortunate when he had cardio planned, as all he wanted was to run alone across the open plains, with nothing but the vast, empty Rasan horizon in sight, not to slog through mud and cold, wet wild grass.

"Training room it is then," he said to an empty room. He didn't have a problem with running in the rain; to him, it was only water. He just didn't feel like it today. It was unlike him to be so lazy. Then again, his enthusiasm for everything had waned in the past few years. Things had changed so much, as he wandered through life without an obvious purpose.

His brothers had moved on with their lives, increasing the distance between them. He no longer attended family gatherings where everyone celebrated events and accomplishments. His father and his father's mate had a new daughter, but that wasn't what had changed things. Alex loved the girl, who had nothing but a sweet smile and a calm disposition for anyone who approached her. There was no jealousy or animosity towards the child, even though he hardly ever saw her. No, that wasn't his problem at all. After a conflict with the outsiders, his mother had disappeared, leaving a cavernous hole in his life. The rest of the community seemed to have moved on from the event, living with a frivolity he couldn't experience.

Alex could not move past it. No one knew where she was. If she had been killed, they should have felt it, shouldn't they? Her mate, Ivan, insisted she would return, but Alex had already given in to his grief, unable to be soothed by Ivan's assertion. This was the second time he had lost her, and he seemed the only one convinced that this time it was permanent. He had searched for years with nothing to show for his efforts. The only thing that seemed to last was his anger towards everyone around him for their growing apathy.

He pondered the thought as he changed into his running gear.

Moments later, Alex trudged into the training room and saw Paneth on one of the running pads.

"You didn't want to run in the rain either?" Alex asked.

"Oh, I don't care about that. I just want to watch the matches," Paneth answered, pointing to the screen in front of his pad.

"That doesn't look like any contest I've seen. What are they playing at?" Alex looked at the display, puzzled.

"I'm not exactly certain. It's an ancient game they used to engage in on one of the Terran planets, T-2866. They call it Earth. Like there aren't already a million planets named after dirt. Regardless, the contest has various names in different districts on the planet.

It's most widely called foot ball. Some places call it soccer and call a totally different, more brutal game, which seems to have nothing to do with striking a ball, foot ball. Either way, it's fascinating." Paneth nodded toward the screen, then screamed. "What in all hells?! How could he miss that? There's nothing in his way!" He enunciated his words by striking out at the air in front of him.

"Why are there only males on the field?" Alex asked, curiously. "When I was on Earth, I only saw a few sporting events with my brothers and Ivan. I do think they called that one football too, but it was a different game."

"Well, as close as I can figure, they separated their contests by gender at first. I've observed games with all female combatants and they're much more vicious. It is possible the males couldn't compete at the beginning," Paneth guessed. He really had no idea why male and female teams would be separated, especially since they didn't seem to play against each other either.

"What about now? Do they still have these contests? Maybe I'll make a stop there while I am on leave. I'd like to see one of these competitions played live. You know we still have a cabin on 2866, but I don't remember much about sport on the planet," Alex admitted.

"Alex, they don't play anything on that planet anymore. There was a massive underwater earthquake caused by the sea floor collapsing into a void underneath, created from excessive petroleum extraction. All the ice caps collapsed into the oceans at once, prompting enormous tidal waves and flooding the whole thing almost ten years ago. There's scarcely any land left and not many hominids, either."

"I went on a fishing trip there a decade or so ago. It doesn't seem realistic. Even if all the ice caps melted, the sea rise would barely be three to four-hundred feet. It wouldn't all be underwater. Are you sure you're thinking of the right planet?"

Alex knew overpopulation had plunged the planet into some rough ecological shape, but he thought they had been working toward solutions. It should have been getting better.

"You mean your *fishing trip*, where you disappeared for a whole year and came back pouting like a little wabbie?" Paneth glanced teasingly at Alex.

Alex rolled his eyes and gestured in front of him to start his pad.

Paneth smirked. "Yeah, I'm sure. Most of the inhabitants evacuated to colonies on Mars, Europa, and Ganymede. They still haven't mastered the technology to get to habitable planets outside of their own sol system yet, but they were able to engineer stable atmospheres and melt ice into water on the places they could reach." Paneth swiped at the screen, pausing the game he was watching. "Here, look at this," he said, bringing up an image narrative of the evacuation procedure.

"If they were able to do all of that, why didn't they fix the planet they already lived on?"

Paneth could only guess at an answer. "Because humans are wasteful. Why would they fix something they broke when they can get themselves something new?"

Alex didn't know the answer to that question either. He turned his attention to the images on the screen.

There wasn't any information in the broadcast on the current state of whatever remained. The only mention was a short section about the residual population squabbling over supplying resources to the outer colonies. Terran protesters were angered over being expected to support colonies of people who ruined their planet and abandoned it.

Alex ran as he watched in silence. He couldn't say it shocked him humans had practically destroyed such a perfect sphere in a short time span. They were still such a primitive, greedy and completely oblivious species for the most part. They were probably astonished that the planet was fighting to save itself from them. As he read, he decided he wanted to see what had happened for himself. He had visited numerous times over the last few centuries and there were people on that planet he had attachments to.

"I guess I've decided where I'm taking my retreat." Alex swiped Paneth's screen to the side, opening his own screen in front of him. He started researching the current climate and remaining land masses as best he could. Most of the information he wanted wasn't available in the current record, but should be in the planetary archives. Alex loathed doing archive research. In actuality, he loathed any type of research. He would go talk to Viv instead. Earth was her origin planet and her brother Vito still lived there the last he heard.

In Alex's memory, the old cabin was high enough in the mountains that it should still be there, even after massive tidal waves. With Rasan technology securing the cabin, there was little chance anyone outside of the turned would be able to occupy it. There was an even slimmer chance any human with device access was alive and remained behind when humans evacuated. Alex contemplated his options. His overwhelming need to know what happened was drawing him there. This had a chance to be a welcome distraction from his monotonous existence.

Paneth shook his head, reviving the sports match he had previously been watching. "That's not what I would consider a vacation," he muttered.

"C'mon Paneth. It's exciting. How often do you get to see the rebirth of a planet and the resurgence of an, albeit primitive species? When was the last time you firsthand witnessed a species on the precipice of venturing outside of their own sol system for the first time? I can't not go to see it for myself." Alex didn't want Paneth to know the underlying reason he was going was personal. The reason he was moody and despondent when he came back the last time had been personal, too.

Paneth couldn't see what was so important to Alex about this planet, although he was aware of a historical element regarding the origin of their species. Those events took place centuries ago. Paneth preferred keeping the past in the past. He couldn't see why Alex enjoyed spending time in a place where his mother used to live, either. To Paneth, those ventures only brought up painful memories, which is why he only visited his home planet of Jur when it was absolutely necessary, and always at the insistence of his father, who Paneth still blamed for his own mother's death.

Alex stepped off the running pad and ported out without saying anything, leaving Paneth alone, shaking his head.

CHAPTER TWO

"Viv?" Alex shouted as he walked down the open hall of a seemingly empty building. He was positive she was here. He had ported to her signature. A descendant could always locate their sire by tracking their genetic signature.

"Viv!" he exclaimed loudly as he passed many unoccupied workstations.

There was an open door at the end of the hall leading to Viv's office. Alex entered and saw Vivienne talking with a young woman he didn't recognize. Vivienne turned her head toward him, raising an accusing brow.

"Alex? What could be so urgent that you would indulge in such uncivil behavior?" Vivienne questioned, as her brow furrowed even more.

"I'm, um," Alex said. "Excuse me, Madame Vivienne."

"Wait in the corridor. I'll be done in a moment," Vivienne answered, adding a sweeping motion of her hand.

Alex took a step backward into the corridor. He leaned against the wall, his hands in the pockets of his running shorts. He felt uncomfortable that he had been so casual with her in front of a stranger. She was the elected Administrator of the turned community on Rasa. The only ones that referred to her as Viv were family and a select few close friends. No one else ever dared. Not because of her position, but out of respect for her as a person. She possessed an air of regality. Alex chuckled to himself at that thought, seeing as he and his brothers were descended from actual royalty. Viv seemed to embody the poise and grace of it, whereas Alex couldn't care less.

A short time later, the young woman raced out of the office, glancing in Alex's direction and smirking as she did so. It wasn't a malicious smirk, simply one that indicated she found the situation amusing. He pushed himself away from the wall and peered around the corner.

"Come on then, tell me what is so pressing." Viv slouched in her chair, her feet on the table in front of her, and sipped her tea. Her demeanor was diametrically opposed to the formality with which she spoke with the young woman.

Alex sheepishly took the chair opposite her. "Viv, I didn't mean to …"

Vivienne fluttered her hand, cutting him off. "No, no. Not necessary. Tell me. What brings my favorite sired son to see me?"

"Viv, I'm your only sired son," Alex said, tilting his head and smirking.

"Well, then you must be my favorite," Viv replied with a sly grin. "Now, what's going on?" She sat up and placed her tea on the table, giving him her full attention.

Alex leaned forward, his elbows resting on his knees. "What happened to your Earth, and why did no one tell me?"

Vivienne let out a laugh that caught Alex off guard. "Why would anyone tell you specifically? It's part of the Planetary Records Archive. Everyone has access to it." His interest in the event was incomprehensible to her. Maybe there had been more to his last visit than he had admitted to.

"What about the old ones - our ancestors? We have a community on this planet." Alex thought it would be better to ask about the turned ones who had stayed behind. He was genuinely concerned about them, even if they weren't his primary focus.

"And we still do. When humans abandoned it rather than face the consequences of what they had been significantly responsible for, our kind, along with other abilitied species, flourished. They no longer hide in the shadows. They have a harmonious relationship with the natural world around them," she explained, knowing that she wasn't answering the question he was really asking.

"Weren't there humans that stayed behind?"

"Some, but not in significant numbers." Vivienne shrugged casually, as she took an interest in his discomfort. He so rarely cared about anything these days. She found it curious.

Alex got up and walked toward the window, considering his next question. He kept his back to Vivienne as he spoke. "Are there any historical documents? Of the populations that fled, and those that stayed behind?"

"Alex, do you think me so oblivious? Do you think I don't already know your thoughts and feelings?" Vivienne was tiring of this dance.

He turned to face her. "No. Not at all."

Vivienne jumped out of her chair to face him. "When you came back, you were sulking. What you really want to know is what happened to a girl."

Alex scoffed. "No!" he protested. "What makes you think there was a girl?"

"Alex," Vivienne said in a sympathetic but slightly condescending tone. "There's always a girl with you. You may be a hundred times my age, but you are notoriously immature. Is that what happens when you're born without fear of natural death? You never grow up?"

He sighed.

Vivienne put her hand on his shoulder and led him over to the bar. "So, this girl, she spurned you, yes?" Vivienne poured two glasses of wine and handed him one.

Alex sighed again. "She didn't think I was serious enough," he paused. "Or reliable enough. Or maybe just not enough." He lowered his eyes dejectedly.

"Oh, Alex." Vivienne chuckled sympathetically. "Human lives are short. There comes a time when they want a mate. They want commitment."

"Things were nice the way they were," he replied.

"That's the downside of a brief life. Time moves faster for them. Life is rushed. Their need to partner is rushed." Vivienne walked back to the windows and took in the view. She remembered being human.

Alex moved beside her. "No one had ever done that to me before. I was heartbroken."

"That woman had summarily dismissed you. You were hurt. You weren't heartbroken. You've as much as admitted you didn't love her. No one likes rejection, even if you already know it will not work out."

Alex didn't reply. Vivienne tilted her head to study him.

"Let me ask you a question," she said after a few moments.

Alex shrugged.

"If you had not known what happened to the planet, would you have ever gone back to look for her?"

Alex thought before answering. "No," he said, shaking his head slowly.

"Then why are you thinking about it now?"

"Because she might be dead." Alex turned to face Vivienne.

"In a hundred years, she would definitely be dead." Vivienne raised her voice a little. She really wanted to yell at him, but felt that would be too harsh.

"Even if I didn't want to see her again, I don't want her to die before her time."

"You have no control over other people's time, Alex. If you really need to see for yourself, don't go with any expectations. Don't go thinking you're going to rekindle a relationship that wasn't right in the first place out of some kind of nostalgia or guilt or because it's convenient for you. That wouldn't be fair to either of you, least of all to her. When you find the right partner, you know it. You would give up everything for them. You would die a hundred deaths for them." Vivienne spoke with old-world Italian passion, locking eyes with him to drive her point home. She took a calming breath and returned to her usual stalwart posture.

Alex chuckled to himself. Vivienne had very specific ideas about what love should be and what it shouldn't be. He couldn't argue with her because he had no experience. He had never felt strongly about anyone outside of his family.

"I promise I won't have any expectations. Whatever the outcome, I want to know." Alex felt better after talking with Vivienne. She had a way of making things clearer to him.

"I'll let Vito know you're coming. Check in with him when you get there, and he'll register you at the Regent's office. Things are different there now. If you have any problems, call Vito right away. Do not try to handle anything on your own. Is that clear?" Vivienne asked firmly.

"Very clear." Alex leaned over and kissed her cheek.

Vivienne scowled at him. Alex could be unpredictable, especially lately. She could only hope that he wouldn't do anything stupid. "Go. I have work to do," she said, pushing him away. "Talk to Harmon. He'll set you up with a suitable shuttle."

"A shuttle? Why wouldn't I use the port to get there?" Alex asked.

"As I said, things are different. You'll want inconspicuous transportation while you're there," Vivienne offered, tilting her chin up at him.

"If we're open with the other species, what difference would my method of transportation make?"

"We are open with them as ordinary turned. You are something different from what they understand, and the old ones don't need to be forced to explain your enhanced abilities. Do I make myself clear?" Vivienne raised her eyebrows to make her point.

"Yes, ma'am. Oh, and thank you," Alex replied with a smile.

Vivienne snapped around and moved briskly away from him, waving her hand dismissively. "Get out, and don't barge into my office again."

"You knew I was coming." Alex flashed his most charming smile and ported out.

A few hours later, Alex went out to the Mechanical Engineering floor to look for Harmon. After a short search, he found him.

"When did you get transferred down here? I thought you only worked with Sadie?" Alex asked.

"I didn't, and I do," Harmon replied, sounding a little annoyed.

"Then why exactly should I see you about a shuttle?" Alex asked further.

"Vivienne and I go way back. I think she's more comfortable asking me for a favor than sending down a priority construct order. She doesn't like to use her position that way." Harmon hypothesized.

"That doesn't make me more comfortable."

"It shouldn't," Harmon laughed and patted Alex on the back. "I have a team. I just lay out the specs. They do all the real work."

Alex breathed a sigh of relief. "You had me there for a minute."

"I try. Let's get you on your way."

CHAPTER THREE

The ship jumped to a point just outside of the galaxy humans referred to as the Milky Way. Silly name for a galaxy, really. He needed to scan for the best spot to come out undetected within the sol system. He finally slipped in under an asteroid close to Saturn until Sadie could generate a suitable signature for his shuttle. Going in cloaked wasn't a good idea. He didn't want to draw attention or to be questioned once he landed regarding where his ship had appeared from. There were two carriers in orbit. Sadie broadcast matching signals for the opposing ships, leading each to believe he had originated from the other one. He entered the planet's approach gate using the ship code originating on Io. Where he was going, the grid had been evacuated to Europa, which would make it easier for him to tell anyone with questions that he had been in Portugal or Italy at the time of the evacuation. It was simple for Sadie's AI network to fool the less sophisticated technology.

His shuttle slipped from behind the asteroid and jumped under one of the carriers, giving him his first view of the planet below. Most of the low-lying coastal areas were gone, but nowhere near as much as he had expected from Paneth's exaggerated description. The continents had shifted quite a bit, but overall, it seemed to be in good shape. Asia and Africa were separated, India was an island of its own. Australia had slid to the south, and he could see that the ice caps at both poles had partially reformed. As the shuttle turned, he could see that the west coast of North America and much of the Baja Peninsula were gone. The land looked like it had been broken off and slid over the shelf, not that it had been covered in place by water. What remained were a few mountain peaks, well west of their original positions, that now appeared to be barrier islands.

Alaska and the northeastern part of Russia had smashed together, both partially separating from their original continents to form a new one. North and South America had split below Mexico, and the southern continent appeared to have flipped over onto Brazil, sliding further into the southern hemisphere. As he finished his pass, he could see that the east coast of the Confederation of States began in Georgia and ended at the tip of Virginia. North of that, along the Great Lakes in the Unified States, a rift had opened deep into Canada, shifting the land northward. He thought it looked like an enormous gaping mouth with Maine for a nose. Islands dotted the inside and out into the ocean like a wet cough with spittle spewing outward. Greenland looked like it was trying to escape the whole mess by pushing its southern part toward Iceland. Ireland, Great Britain, and Europe had shifted slightly to the south and appeared to have been elevated, gaining land, and closing the gap between Northern Ireland and Scotland.

The atmosphere was much clearer than the last time he was here. Major coastal cities had been shattered and swept away, replaced by lush new foliage and rocky beaches. The inland cities were mostly reduced to rubble, abandoned and overgrown, with few signs of humanoid life, yet teaming with revived animal species. The populated areas he could make out from this height were scattered across the landscape rather than towering over each other, reminiscent of the farming villages of the Old Worlds.

Alex descended over the east coast of North America before turning back towards the Rocky Mountains. It was agonizing for him to keep his shuttle at such a slow speed, but he didn't want to draw attention to himself. The capabilities of the Terran ships were much reduced from the speeds he was used to. It gave him a good view of the luxurious, vibrant landscape below, so he didn't complain. It was part of what he had come to see. As he approached the cabin, he could see small communities dotting the region. There were signs of life, but not as overwhelmingly abundant as before.

The shuttle began its descent into the open area in front of the cabin's garage. The house appeared to be in good condition. It was a bit run down, but considering what the planet had been through, he expected it to be much worse. Alex climbed out of the shuttle and took a deep breath of the clean, fresh air. The last time he had been here, it had been smoggy all the way up into the mountains. It was an unexpected relief that the air had become so much clearer once the plants had filled in. It wasn't as clean as the air on Rasa, but it was better than he could remember Earth ever being. He stepped down, feeling the old gravel crunch under a blanket of new moss. As he walked up the steps to the porch, he felt them give a few inches under his weight. The porch boards creaked and echoed under his footsteps. He turned to look at the scene down the old driveway and across the mountaintops. A faint smile crept across his face as he remembered spending the best year of his life in this house. Slowly, the smile faded as memories of how it had ended took over.

Alex sighed and turned to open the door. The biometric lock responded to his touch with a series of lights showing that the port blocker was offline. It flashed another set of lights, allowing him to enter. He would have to deal with this problem later, he thought as stale air wafted towards him, causing him to sneeze. The house had been shuttered, but he couldn't tell for how long. Maybe years, maybe weeks. He walked through the kitchen, opening blinds and windows on his way to the back deck. The first thing on the agenda was a proper cleaning, he thought to himself. He opened the doors and flipped on the light switch. The power was on, which meant the energy generator was working. Next, he checked the water. Hot and cold were both working and running clear, which could only mean that someone had maintained it.

It smelled unpleasant to his heightened senses, prompting him to consider changing the air and water filters. He went outside around the back of the house to the maintenance cellar entrance. Everything was still where it should be in the mechanical room under the house. He removed the air filters and cleaned them in the sanitizer before replacing the water filter with a new one from the shelf. He tossed the old filter into the recycling box and heard it clatter against something. When he pulled the box out to look, there were nine used filters inside, nine years' worth. It had been empty when he left. He clearly remembered dropping them off at the recyclers the last time he and Gen went skiing, because it was also the last day he was here. A dull ache radiated from his chest as he stared into the box. It was obvious to him that someone had stayed here and taken care of the place. Of course, they had a caretaker, but he had been human. It was more likely he had left with the others, and someone else had occupied the house right after the catastrophic events. Could it have been Gen who stayed here after he left? He needed to go back to the house to look around.

When Alex returned to the main floor, he could see dust particles swirling through the beams of sunlight and decided that looking and cleaning could be done together. The kitchen would be the right place to start. Cleaning reminded him of the first time he had come to the cabin with Ivan and his brothers, which made him smile. He noticed nothing was covered in dirt. Perhaps only a few months' worth of dust had collected, and no mold or residue. Given the life span of the air filters, Alex calculated that the place had been uninhabited for three to six months if none had ever been dropped at the recyclers again. That was long enough for it to be unkempt, but not long enough for it to have deteriorated.

As he finished downstairs, he remembered he hadn't checked in with Vito upon his arrival.

Alex pulled his TAC out of his pocket and entered the code Vivienne had given him for Vito.

"Victor Costa," Vito said.

"Hey Vito, it's Alex," he said, upon hearing the familiar, rich Italian accent.

"Alex! How was the trip?" Vito asked.

"Slow. I'm not used to taking so much time to get around one tiny little planet."

Vito laughed at him. "Isn't that the point of a vacation? To slow down."

"Yeah, I guess."

"Well, that doesn't sound so convincing. Of all the planets in The Everything you could have chosen from, why did you come back here if you didn't want to relax?" Vito asked.

"Curiosity, I guess. I just wanted to see what had happened. The planet has undergone some significant changes."

"I know. I was here. And that is a complete bullshit answer if I ever heard one. You could have gotten all the information you wanted from Sadie, or you could have called if you were so curious."

"I should have called, but I didn't know until a few days ago," Alex said.

"Alex, we have received a significant amount of support from the community on Rasa. If you didn't know what was going on here, it was because you didn't want to know. I understand. Viv told me you didn't want any news about Earth when you got back."

"It's true. I didn't want to hear about it. Genevieve broke my heart before I left," Alex replied, feeling sorry for himself.

Vito scoffed. "You are only fooling yourself, Alex. You haven't thought about that girl in ten years. Women queue up for you and you go through them as fast as they get in line. She didn't break your heart; she bruised your ego."

"Why would you say that? You don't know what she meant to me," Alex said, with a defensive edge to his voice.

"Because I know what love is, and that was not love. You are romanticizing the relationship because now you feel guilty. If you loved her, you would have checked on her. You would have known what was happening here and you would have known whether she was safe or not. No, it was not love, but she did hurt you. She ended things, and you finally got to feel what it was like to be cast aside instead of the other way around." Vito paused. "Tell me I am wrong."

Alex couldn't respond. What Vito had said was true. After a few weeks back on Rasa, he hadn't thought of her again until two days ago. That realization saddened him. He didn't think of himself as cold-hearted but thought he must be. He sighed.

Vito scoffed gently this time. "Do not be too hard on yourself. You live your life wide open, accepting what comes and goes without attachment. Some people are like that."

Alex didn't want to be like that. He wanted to make deeper connections with others. "Do you think you can find out what happened to her?" he asked.

"I can try. No promises though, eh? After the Exodus, there was a gap in some human historical records. It may not be possible."

"I understand. Thanks Vito." His mood was solemn as he ended the call. Vito had summed him up in one phrase: open and without attachment. Outside of his family, he really didn't have any attachments. Maybe Paneth, he thought. Paneth had become a good friend over the past centuries. Alex would be very sad if something happened to him. How could he not have noticed that he had become so self-centered? His mother always said he was the sensitive one. That may have been true in the distant past, before he had lost so much.

He couldn't change what had happened in the past, but he could clean up the home and make it the place of comfort he remembered. He made his way down to the wine cellar, pulling out a half cask of scotch, turned on some music, and began his task.

CHAPTER FOUR

Alex awoke to a band of bright sunlight streaming across his face. His neck was twisted in an odd direction, his head half dangling from the sofa. Cold air from the open window negated any warmth that would have come from the morning sun. He reached for his t-shirt lying on the floor beside him and brought it up to his face to sniff. It was still damp with sweat and smelled musty. He curled his lip and tossed the shirt aside as he rolled off the sofa with an old man's groan and stumbled toward the kitchen. His belt hung unevenly off to one side, weighing down the wrinkled pants before catching on his hips. He stumbled over the pooled material around his feet, jerked the belt loose, and tossed it behind him.

"Sadie, coffee," he slurred, to no response. His confusion was palpable. It took Alex a few seconds to remember that they used an older form of artificial assistance in the cabin for personal services.

A limited version of Sadie had been installed solely for physical security.

"Ida, coffee, black." Alex finally said, shaking his head rapidly to clear the cobwebs. He wasn't a morning person like his brother Mikkel, who was far too cheerful in the early hours. Even a sleep pod couldn't elevate Alex's demeanor in the morning.

"Good morning, Alex," Ida greeted. "There is no coffee available in the convenience system. Would you like to substitute hot tea?"

Alex groaned. He hadn't considered that he would have to go shopping while he was here. The food supply had been automated before. "Tea is fine, Ida, with milk."

Ida replied, "There is no milk in the refrigeration compartment of the convenience system."

Of course not, he thought. There wouldn't be anything perishable left. Ida would have disposed of everything that spoiled.

"Black tea is fine, Ida," he finally replied.

The convenience panel produced an empty cup, and he could hear the water boiling inside. Two minutes later, he watched as the dark brown beverage appeared. He took the cup and gulped it down, wincing. It was hot, but that wasn't the reason for the negative reaction. It was stale.

"Uck. Ida, purge the tea leaves from the convenience system." He would go get some fresh ones after he showered.

"Purge all the tea leaves, Alex, or just the used ones?"

"All tea leaves," Alex said. "And send an inventory to my TAC."

A few seconds later, the device in his pocket vibrated, indicating receipt of the requested inventory. Ignoring it, he stumbled upstairs, anticipating a long, hot shower.

The master bedroom was almost exactly as he remembered it. Almost. The room was large, dark, and smelled of death. Not a bloody, violent death. It smelled like the long, drawn-out death of age and disease. It smelled … sad. That was the only word that came to mind. It was one thing to die in a glorious, bloody battle with passion and adrenaline coursing through your veins. He had tasted that type of death many times. It was a brave death that released your consciousness from its physical shell, freeing you to be reborn. That kind of death was celebrated. What he smelled here was an end in pain, illness, and weakness. One that slowly slides over you, diminishing everything about you. One you knew was coming and had no way of avoiding. One that resulted in a permanent end, a mortal end. Alex had never witnessed such a death himself. From the stories he heard, it was one he never wanted to see.

He shook off the thought and switched on the light. The heavy curtains were drawn, and the lights created a dim, dreary atmosphere. The air filters had done their job and removed the staleness from the air, although he would still need to clean the room at some point if he was going to stay here. Alex ran a hand through his hair and trudged across the oppressive space to the bathroom. There were no personal items to be found. The room looked as if everything had been taken away. There wasn't even soap. He sighed, remembering that he had left his bag downstairs. On his way back down, he passed by the hall bathroom and stuck his head in. Score! He thought and triumphantly grabbed a flowery-smelling bar of hand-cut soap before heading back to the other bathroom. He smiled to himself. Gen would have strangled him if she had caught him using her special decorative "guest soap."

After a very long, very hot shower, Alex was wide awake and in a much better mood. He grabbed his dirty pants off the floor and pulled out his TAC before tossing the pants into the sanitizer. Thirty seconds later, he pulled them out and smelled them. Satisfied with the cleanliness, he put them on and began humming and dancing his way downstairs. He stopped midway down, realizing he wasn't alone. His inattention made it too late for a stealthy entry, and before he had time to react, a figure sped toward him from the kitchen.

"Alex! There you are," the figure stopped and spoke.

Alex dropped his defensive posture and slowly walked down the remaining stairs. "You shouldn't sneak up on people, Alonzo. I could have killed you."

"I would be honored to be temporarily dispatched by you," Alonzo said with an exaggerated bow that made Alex laugh. Alonzo's once thick Italian accent had diminished since the last time Alex had seen him.

"Whatever it is, it can't be good news if Vito sent you to tell me in person. Is Gen dead?" Alex asked.

Alonzo nodded. "Yes, but it's a little more complicated than that."

"Well then, I hope you brought coffee."

"Get dressed," Alonzo said, taking a clean shirt from the bag at the foot of the stairs, and throwing it at Alex. "We'll go back to the vineyard where you can have some real caffè and a decent breakfast." Alonzo's eyes scanned the convenience machine with lights flashing "empty".

Alex pulled the shirt over his head. "Must be some really bad news if I'm being called in."

Alonzo shrugged and waited for Alex to lace up his boots. As soon as he finished, the duo walked outside and ported back to the vineyard, where Vito greeted them. Alonzo and Alex followed Vito into the dining room, where two women were already eating and talking. Alex recognized them as Isabella and Corinna, Spanish sisters who were on the Board.

"Oh, this is an ambush, then. What rule have I broken now?" Alex glanced at Vito, wondering what was going on.

"Don't be daft," Isa waved Alex off. "We came this morning to exchange pears and figs for wine."

Cori pushed her chair back. "Your narcissist is showing, dear. Might want to tuck that in around here," she teased, hopping up to give him a kiss on the cheek and scratch at the scruff on his chin. "This is new."

Alex lowered his head in embarrassment. "I was trying to appear older. I didn't know who was going to see me."

"You don't have to do that here anymore. There are more species left behind with abilities than humans now. We all embrace each other's nature," Isa said.

Vito sat at the head of the table, motioning Alex and Alonzo to sit. Alex hadn't realized how hungry he was until he smelled the food. He hadn't eaten since he left Rasa the morning before. He filled his plate, savoring a rich cup of cappuccino with his meal.

"Alonzo told me that Gen is dead. What, may I ask, was he not telling me?" Alex asked between bites.

"Mato also died three months ago," Alonzo answered.

"It's tragic that he outlived his daughter. I don't quite see where this is going."

"A week before Mato died, he contacted the World Orphanage for Abilitied Children," Alonzo continued carefully.

Alex grew irritated with the slow drip of information. "Oh, for the love of Prometheus! Just say it already!"

"She had a child," Vito said flatly.

"Good for her. What does that have to do with me?"

"The child is nine and a half," Alonzo interjected.

"So, she threw me out because she cheated on me and got pregnant?" Alex's brow furrowed in disappointment.

"Just because the child is the right age doesn't mean it's his," Isa added, tilting her head sideways.

"That's where your mind goes, Alex? She just happened to cheat on you with another vampire in a world full of humans and you couldn't smell it on her?" Cori scoffed.

Alex winced at the word vampire. On Rasa, that word was considered a filthy slur and had been stricken from their language centuries ago. Undeterred by her crude insult, he responded angrily, "Yeah, that's where my mind goes. I couldn't have gotten her pregnant. I never turned off my inhibitor, and I never got an alert that it was malfunctioning. All my scans are normal. I don't care what any of you think. It can't be mine." It was clear to him where this was headed, and he couldn't help but feel a sense of unease. He wasn't going to let them make him take responsibility for someone else's child. As anger surged through him, he stood up forcefully.

"Where are the scans of the child? That will prove it. Compare them to mine!"

Vito motioned for him to return to his seat. Alex reluctantly complied.

Alonzo began with hesitation. "There aren't any."

"HA!" exclaimed Alex.

Alonzo continued, "The only previous record we have of a child in this family was from the evacuation. Genevieve presented herself at the evacuation site and the records show that she said she was three months pregnant. Examinations show she was close to gestational term, and she was disqualified for travel because she had, and I quote, 'rapidly deteriorating health deemed unsurvivable for travel'." Alonzo checked the record for the wording. "The gestation period is consistent with our species and no other we can find, and the child was draining her."

"Which is why mating with a human was forbidden by the community in the first place," Isa shrugged casually. "It usually kills them."

"That's enough, Isa. This is my house, and I didn't invite your politics into the conversation," Vito shot her a warning look.

"This still doesn't prove anything. It certainly doesn't prove it was mine. How do you know that child even survived, or Gen, for that matter? You said yourself she died. What makes you think that Mato even handed over the same child? He could have taken in an orphan himself after the Exodus." Alex still had enough doubts to support his argument. He was not about to go claim responsibility for a child which, in his mind, absolutely could not be his.

"Well, for one thing, Mato said the child was his grandchild, and he had no reason to lie. If the child was human, they wouldn't have accepted it at WOAC. Second, Genevieve survived the birth. She didn't die until seven years later from a mountain lion attack. We have a death certificate for her," Vito said, keeping a calm demeanor. He locked eyes with Alex, whose mouth was open. "And third, it doesn't matter whether the child is yours or not. If it is a member of this community and you can claim parental rights, you will claim that child."

"Or what?" Alex shot back defiantly.

Isa and Cori exchanged a worried look.

Vito sighed. "Alex, no one is saying you have to raise this child yourself. We can find a suitable home. What we can't do is leave a turned child out there alone with no understanding of what it is. What's going to happen when the child reaches puberty and its canis come in? Think about what happened with Lilly. And she had the ability to travel, to bond, to educate herself. She was with others like her. Do you really think a child deserves to grow up lost like that? If there is any possibility that this child is yours, who knows what other dangerous abilities it might have? Others could get hurt. This is not about you. All we ask is that you make the claim. We'll take care of the rest."

Cori added her reasoning to the conversation. "The Board will make sure the child is taken care of when you file the claim."

Vito glared in her direction. She may be on the board, but in his house, she had no standing, and her interference was more likely to push Alex off than anything else.

Alex was frustrated. Did he have a child out there that he never knew about and didn't want? Did Gen think so little of him and not even tell him? Or was this someone else's child, abandoned and alone? He clenched his fists and pushed himself away from the table. The room had suddenly become too small. Everyone was staring at him. He left the claustrophobic confinement of the villa, shaking his head. Alonzo started to go after him when Vito grabbed his arm.

"Give him a minute. It's a lot to work through."

Alex sat on the old vineyard wall and chucked stones into the field below. He thought back to the day she broke off their relationship. They had gone skiing. He thought they were having a great time. The entire day was seared into his memory. Waking up at five in the morning. Stopping by the recyclers. Breakfast at that little coffee shop she liked to stop at, followed by hours on the slopes. They laughed all day before ending up in front of the immense stone fireplace at the lodge.

"Aww, look Alex, isn't she adorable?" Gen asked, pointing to a little girl who was feeding a smaller child scoops of whipped cream from her cup of hot chocolate as they giggled at each other.

"Yeah, but for every one of those, you get ten of these," Alex replied, pointing to a group of children fighting, screaming, and generally misbehaving.

"I think that says more about the parents than the kids." Gen pointed back and forth, comparing the adults. The parents of the happy children were laughing with them, giving them their full attention and encouragement, while the other parents were immersed in their digital devices, ignoring their unruly brood.

"With the overpopulation on this planet, there is no good reason to have them anyway," he said nonchalantly.

"Don't you ever want children?" Gen asked.

"Hells no! I like living in the moment, like we are now. I don't have to worry about anyone except myself. I do what I want and spend time with whomever I want. It's perfect." Alex pulled her onto his lap and nuzzled her neck. "This is perfect," he purred into her ear.

She didn't answer him. It was the only conversation they had about children in his memory. It must have been enough, because on the drive home, she ended their relationship. She calmly explained that they were too different. They wanted different things out of life, and she had no hope that he would ever grow up and become a responsible adult. Gen wasn't mean or angry or any of the other things he expected. She didn't fight with him or beg him to change like some girls did when he broke up with them. She was just firm in the thought that they didn't have a future and it would be easiest for both of them if he were gone before she woke up in the morning.

It was an interesting situation when he thought back. It was his house she was kicking him out of, and he didn't care. Her father had been the caretaker for their family since before Gen was born. The two of them lived in a small house at the other end of the property, so this seemed to be their home as much as Alex's. Even more so, considering the amount of time his family had spent there over the years compared to hers.

Alex struggled with making the decision. If he claimed the child as his own, he would be admitting that Gen had already decided that he wasn't good enough to be in her life. She had decided that he didn't have enough redeeming qualities to even tell him that he was going to be a parent. She had judged him incapable without even giving him a choice. It was very likely he would have chosen not to stay, but he would have been able to provide support. He could have had some involvement or input into how the child was raised. The child would have been aware of the community and received help in grasping the concept of being born turned. The child would have grown up in a better situation with a family. He should have had a choice.

Alonzo came out and sat on the wall next to Alex, interrupting his thoughts. He picked up a stone and skipped it across a large rock at the edge of the field, propelling it over several rows of dormant vines.

"I know what he wants," Alex said, without looking at Alonzo. "He says he just wants me to claim the child, but he wants me to raise it. He wants me to take responsibility and settle down. He thinks that would be good for me. No doubt he's talked to Vivienne." Alex continued pitching rocks so hard they dug several feet into the ground, while Alonzo skipped stones with elegant precision and remained silent.

"You don't get it!" Alex threw another stone that landed in an explosion of dust which traveled across the field like a low cloud. "None of them have a clue. My whole life has been about serving others. Ever since my grandfather realized my brothers and I could fight, it's been 'go quell this rebellion, go conquer this planet, go here, go there, do this, do that.' We never had a moment of freedom until we were turned." Alex threw another stone.

"I cannot raise this child because I will spend the entire time resenting it. I finally got a taste of what it's like to live for myself. I couldn't look at this child without seeing it as another weighted chain around my neck, pulling me down. I don't want to feel that way, but I can't help it. I would be a terrible parent because I don't want to be a parent. It wouldn't be fair to either of us," Alex said, looking defeated.

Alonzo could sympathize with his friend, even if he couldn't understand his point of view. This vineyard had been Alonzo's home since childhood, where his parents and Vito raised him with love and care. He had never lived anywhere else because he never wanted to be anywhere else. He had an entire community here to encourage and support him in finding his own path.

"That is a decision you have to make for yourself *after* you get the child out of that place. The child doesn't need to know you're its father unless you want it to," Alonzo said, tilting his head to look up at Alex.

Alex sighed deeply. "I know we can't leave the child there. I just wish I wasn't the one who had to go."

CHAPTER FIVE

"Mr. Johnson?"

Alex didn't answer when a voice called out to him. The voice edged closer, becoming louder. "Mr. Johnson."

His head snapped up from the data pad Vito had given him when he realized he was Mr. Johnson. Alex stood up awkwardly and held out his hand to the person who was standing in front of him. "My apologies."

The ward advocate recoiled at the gesture, avoiding eye contact. "We do not make physical contact here unless we are restraining a ward. I have been advised that you are here to claim a child."

"Yes, yes, that's right," Alex stammered, smiling nervously. He had dressed in old, ill-fitting clothing and glasses to take on a meeker appearance. His demeanor was nervous and submissive. The glasses were a calculated touch for obfuscation purposes. The devices were rare, as people in this century had a variety of ways to improve their vision. Most people tended to pay attention to a unique item rather than the wearer of the item. He also had Sadie project his eye color as brown instead of the distinctive green he inherited from his mother. He wanted to be as invisible as possible under the circumstances.

"Claim code," the advocate said in a flat, firm tone.

Alex fumbled with the data pad and brought up the code to be scanned. "May I ask how long the child has been here?"

"You may not request any information until I verify your claim code," the advocate said, as she arched an eyebrow and glowered at him.

Alex flipped the data pad around so the advocate could scan it with another. The pad beeped twice. The advocate turned and began walking toward the secure door adjacent to the reception desk. "Follow me, Mr. Johnson."

Two beeps, Alex thought. Were two beeps good or two beeps bad? It didn't matter. He was only trying it this way as a courtesy to Vito. The alliance between the planet's abilitied species was a little tense due to the changes it had undergone, since humans were no longer the dominant species. He didn't want to add to it unnecessarily. The fact was, no matter how the ruse ended, he was taking the child with him. The sooner he made the claim, the sooner he could put this all behind him and return to his life on Rasa.

"Two days," the advocate said as she opened the security door.

"The child's grandfather died three months ago," Alex said, raising his voice and giving it a harsh edge. Had they left this child out there alone for months with no regard for it?

The advocate ignored his statement. "Place your personal belongings in the box to your left and step through the scanner."

He placed his data pad and ring in the box and stepped through the scanner, which was activated by flashing red lights.

"Visual aids, Mr. Johnson," the advocate pointed at his face.

"I can't see without them," he said.

"You'll get them back once you have been scanned."

He wasn't worried about the scan. They wouldn't be able to interpret his primordial and Æsir DNA anyway, and Sadie was tracking and projecting standard human/vampire sources over it. Sadie would remove anything potentially harmful to the community from their system. He took off the glasses and squinted, contorting his face as he passed through the scanner again. The receptionist pushed the box towards him after the scanner flashed green. Alex stood still, pretending to have limited vision.

"I thought vampires had crazy good eyesight," the receptionist quipped, getting an admonishing glare from the advocate.

"That's a fallacy. Being sired enhances what you already have. I was blind before, so my limited vision is an enhancement." Alex perfectly portrayed the character he had created as he stretched for his glasses. He didn't consider it a lie; it was an act.

"Well, in this day and age, there's no reason not to have your vision corrected," the receptionist retorted, risking the advocate's wrath once again as she placed the glasses in Alex's outstretched hand.

"Ms. Horne! Please keep your opinions to yourself. There is no need to engage in prying conversation." The advocate glared at the younger woman.

"It's not an intrusion," Alex said. He put on the glasses. "When dealing with other species, Ms. Horne, you should consider that not everyone is of this era. Some of us have things we may not be ready to let go of." He took the remaining items from the box.

"Mr. Johnson, you need to leave the data pad. The children have restricted access to outside technology. You can retrieve it when you leave." The advocate instructed him dryly, motioning for him to return it to the box.

"O … Oh, yes. Of course," Alex stammered, quickly returning the item to the box.

When he turned around, the advocate was walking down the hall. He followed her to a large office where several people were meeting. The advocate stopped abruptly a few steps inside the door. Alex clumsily bumped his shoulder into the door frame, deepening his harmless, bumbling persona. The less threatening he appeared, the more likely this transaction would end favorably.

"Miss Winterclaw!" the advocate announced loudly, waving across the room.

A woman turned away from a group she was chatting with and walked toward them. She appeared to be in her early twenties and a little on the thick side for Alex's taste, with shoulder-length curly chestnut hair and deep tanned skin. She wasn't overweight by any means. Her figure was toned yet feminine, and she was almost as tall as he was. There was something about the confident way she carried herself that caught his attention. He suspected it attracted the attention of most men.

"Ma'am?" the woman asked as she approached.

"This is Mr. Johnson. Please escort him to ward 070107 and complete his claim," the advocate said flatly without looking at Alex. She quickly strode away from the pair, leaving him dumbfounded.

"I've never seen her run from anyone so quickly. I think she's afraid of you." The woman smiled and reached out to shake Alex's hand. "I'm Kitty."

The confusion on Alex's face was obvious as he watched the advocate disappear into the crowded room and shook Kitty's hand aimlessly. Her skin was very warm against his.

"Alex. Alex Johnson, pleased to meet you, Kitty. Wait," his attention shifted, "Kitty … Winterclaw? You're a blood wolf named Kitty? Is that not an insult?" Alex could not hide his amusement when he realized what kind of wolf she was, even though he knew it was rude to comment on it.

Kitty curled her lip in a snarl and flashed amber eyes. Alex stepped back, posturing for a confrontation, before Kitty broke into a wide grin accompanied by a warm laugh, dissolving the momentary tension. "Yeah. The irony is not lost on me. One of the pack Gammas used to tell me 'Tigers are kitties too' when the other kids teased me. My wolf was shy and came later than she should have. I learned to accept it." She shrugged. "Come on, let's get started," Kitty nodded her head in the direction of the long hall to her left and started walking in that direction.

Alex breathed a sigh of relief, knowing he hadn't ruined the assignment before it even began with an unnecessary comment. He hadn't really cared when he'd asked. It just seemed too irresistible not to comment. It baffled him she would share so much with a complete stranger, although the idea of finding out more about her wasn't uncomfortable for him. He sensed she was more restless than nervous. Alex shook off the thought and followed her down the corridor.

The first level they walked through had bright rooms with several children in each, monitored from one central desk, reminiscent of a hospital nurse's station. Each room had a clear wall facing the hallway and set activities for the children to engage in. Older children's rooms had an automated companion to guide daily routines. A species-specific adult with several helper companions staffed rooms with younger children.

As they descended, the lower corridors were long and gloomy, lined with row upon row of heavy metal doors. In contrast to the bright, open rooms above, this area, with its inadequate lighting and musty air, more closely resembled a prison than an orphanage. The smell of bleach and mothballs assaulted his sensitive nose. Abrupt sounds of slamming doors and screaming children echoed throughout. The situation unnerved Alex. How could anyone treat these broken, abandoned children this way? He now understood why Vito had insisted on claiming the child. Such negative treatment created the most dangerous creatures, as history has shown time and time again.

"So, what can you tell me about the child?" Alex asked.

"The child? You mean your daughter?" Kitty replied with a sneer.

"Yes. I mean, I didn't know. I didn't know there was a child until yesterday. This is the first time I've been back since the catastrophe. I'm not exactly from around here." Alex stammered. His answer was as honest as he was able to make it.

"Oh," Kitty said in an apologetic tone, lowering her head in embarrassment. "That's not as unusual as you might hope lately. We have a lot of kids here who shouldn't be. I'm sure it's the same where you come from." Kitty paused and lifted her eyes sideways to steal a quick look at his face. "She's the first child of your kind we've encountered. Until you sent the claim request, we didn't know what she was. She doesn't have fangs," she explained, looking him over.

"Those don't come until later for pure born. If she had been born into a clan, she wouldn't have been away from her mother until after puberty." Alex said, wincing at the fang reference. "A scan should have shown what she was." The thought of them scanning her hadn't occurred to him before now. His stomach flipped when he said it, but he wanted to know if they had.

Kitty flashed a withering smile and changed the subject.

"Most of the staff are afraid of her." Kitty turned her head fully and locked eyes with him.

"But not you?"

Kitty shook her head. "I'm afraid *for* her."

"I don't understand." Alex said, leaning toward her.

Kitty looked over her shoulder and exhaled. With her breath, her entire body sagged like a deflating balloon. Alex could tell she was conflicted, watching her eyes dart as she searched for the right words.

"She was born into a human world. Everyone she knew is dead, and I don't think she understands what she is." Kitty fixed her eyes on him again. "She's scared, and she's angry, and she's very, very strong. But that's not the unusual part. Most of these kids are like that to some degree."

"Then what's the unusual part?" Alex pressed.

"She doesn't speak. I don't know if she can't or just won't. I can't even tell if she understands everything that's said to her, because she doesn't always react to it in a way that you would consider normal. She's in her own little bubble. I'm afraid that a child like her could be perceived as dangerous. If you hadn't come, I think they would have put her to sleep." Kitty winced at the last part and dropped her eyes to the ground. That was human behavior. Kill what you don't understand. She was ashamed that the people who ran this place would consider that as an option. To make matters worse, to really kill one of the turned, they would have to be burned to ashes. It sickened her to think of intentionally burning a child alive.

"I appreciate your candor." Alex swallowed down emotions that wouldn't serve him here. He couldn't think of anything else to say. He felt heavy. A mixture of guilt and anger, followed by a wave of protectiveness he hadn't expected. He didn't want to feel this way towards the girl. He wanted to remain distant. It would be better for both of them. He repeated to himself that he was only there to claim her. Gen had seen all along that he wasn't father material. Another thought entered Alex's mind and brought him back to the present moment.

"Is that why she's down here? Because they're afraid of her?"

"Among other things." Kitty grinned in a way that didn't quite fit the moment.

"What other things?" Alex asked tentatively, hoping she hadn't killed anyone.

"She's a runner."

Alex exhaled, releasing the pressure from his jaw. "Is that why she's only been here two days when she should have been in the system for three months?"

Kitty stifled a laugh, knowing it might be considered inappropriate. "Yes, she has been in the system for three months, but they can't seem to keep her anywhere she doesn't want to be. She's escaped from every single facility she's been placed in. I have tracked her down at least a dozen times. I think it's become a game for her. Now she runs with my wolf for miles back to the shuttle. I haven't had to dose her since the fourth time I caught her."

"She's formed an attachment to you?" Alex phrased the statement as a question.

"As much as she's capable of right now, I guess."

"So, do you actually work here, or do you just track runners?" Alex asked.

"I'm a tracker. I have an as-needed contract with the department. I was called in to handle Skeat's transfer in case she ran from you."

"Skeat? *That's* her name?" He felt like he should have asked sooner. It was a strange thing to call a girl.

"Oh. God, I'm so sorry. Of course, you didn't know her name. You didn't even know she was a girl."

Alex shook his head. "This is all kind of unusual for me. Skeat, huh? It's a … a nice name," for a boy, he thought to himself.

Kitty shook her head and laughed lightly. "Skeat is just what I call her. She seems to like it, anyway. She's so small and quick, with big eyes that are always watching, like one of those little skink lizards. I didn't think skink was an appropriate nickname, so I settled on Skeat. Her given name is Alexia Grace."

Alex was shaken. His chest tightened as if Kitty had punched him in the throat. His face flushed and his eyes burned as he choked up. All the pain of his mother's disappearance, which had originally prompted his visit to Earth ten years ago, was crashing down on him. This planet had been the end of any hope of finding her after decades of searching The Everything and coming up empty. After many years, the community had lost hope of finding her. They moved on, their nonchalant attitude suggesting that her presence or absence made no difference to them. Alex had come here to escape the suffocating waves of grief that had consumed him. Most of the inhabitants of The Everything did not know what his mother had done for them before she disappeared, but Alex could never forget.

"Are you okay?" Kitty reached out and grasped a deceptively muscular arm hidden beneath the oversized jacket.

Her touch shocked him a little, as if she had dragged her feet across a carpet before grabbing his arm. As his knees buckled, he caught himself against the wall.

"She named her after my mother," he whispered, not realizing he had said it out loud.

What in all hells is wrong with me? he thought, shaking his head. Words caught in his throat, and he struggled to inhale as a wave of breathlessness washed over him. He leaned forward, placing his hands on his knees until he could finally take a deep breath.

From his reaction, Kitty assumed his mother had passed. "I understand. I lost my parents, too." She frowned while closing her eyes in a slow blink.

"These kids are lucky to have understanding people like you," Alex said.

In his mind, it was an attempt to empathize, but it seemed disconnected from the personal experience Kitty had shared. Her parents were gone forever, while he still had hope of seeing his mother again, and his father was very much alive. His thoughts became unfocused, distracted by the unusual effect her touch had on him. Why had he said something so sappy and out of character? Why was he so focused on her fingers grasping his bicep?

"Do you need me to call for assistance?" Kitty asked, pulling him forward. He felt her warmth flow through his arm.

Alex quickly composed himself. "No, no, I'm fine. Not much surprises me, but I wasn't expecting this. A few seconds later, he pushed himself away from the wall and stood up straight.

Kitty pulled her hand away and rubbed it on her pants as if wiping away dirt. She cocked her head and nodded toward the end of the hall. "You ready? It's down there. Last one on the right."

Alex gestured for Kitty to take the lead. "I'm ready." How hard can it be to pick up a kid and get her out of here?

Kitty stopped at the door. She reached up and released the heavy latch with a loud clang. The rusted hinges creaked as she slowly pushed the door inward a few feet and stepped through. Alex turned sideways and slid through behind her. Two meters in front of them was a metal table pushed against a thick polycarbonate wall. They could see Skeat, but she couldn't see them.

"What in all hells have you people done to her?!" Alex yelled at Kitty. The sight of Skeat's condition made him angry.

She was much smaller than he had expected, sitting on the floor in the far corner of an almost empty room. Her curly, matted hair covered most of her face, with bits of leaves and sticks poking through the tight, spiraling curls. Her clothes were filthy and tattered. She looked disheveled and disengaged, like a wild creature that had finally realized it could not escape an impending slaughter. She was staring at something in her hands. He saw her nostrils flare as she caught their scent. Otherwise, she was motionless.

"Nothing. No one can get near her except me, and that's only when she lets me," Kitty said, trying to remain calm. She had prepared herself for the reaction she thought he would have and didn't react to the anger.

"Open the door!" Alex snarled through clenched teeth.

Kitty shook her head no.

"Now!" he roared.

"You can't go in there like that!" Kitty yelled back. "You need to calm down."

"You need to open the fucking door!" he snarled angrily, towering over Kitty as she recoiled from him.

His voice made her flinch. She spontaneously cowered to him as she would to her own Alpha, baring her neck and squeezing her eyes shut. It was an involuntary reaction. She wished she could control it with every fiber of her being. She wished he wouldn't make her feel this way. His anger cut her to the bone. Wincing, she scrambled past him to the lock pad between the two chambers.

He knew he scared her and didn't care. No one deserved to be locked up like an animal, completely isolated, let alone a terrified child with little understanding of what was going on around her.

Kitty opened the door and stepped aside as Alex pushed past her. His pace slowed as he approached Skeat. The child continued to stare into her cupped hands, not acknowledging his presence. He knelt before her, looking for any sign that she was aware of his proximity. His nostrils flared as a foul odor wafted toward him. He wondered how long it had been since she had been bathed, followed by a worse thought, wondering when she had last been fed.

"Skeat?" he said softly, leaning closer.

Skeat's hand closed tight around whatever she had in it as he moved into her peripheral vision. Her body tightened into a petrified, solid stillness. Not a single breath escaped her lips.

"Skeat? Do you know what I am?" Alex asked more quietly as he reached out to touch her arm.

Kitty's eyes widened. She knew what was coming. She felt a certain satisfaction knowing that the arrogant, cynical bastard fully deserved it.

The moment Alex's fingertips brushed Skeat's arm, he felt a jolt of extreme pain in his head, along with the sounds of screaming, laughing, and muttering from every creature within a mile radius of the girl. It was an incredibly loud, confusing jumble of external thoughts and emotions. No wonder she couldn't focus on anything. She had never been taught to block out other people's thoughts. Every single second in this place was sheer torture for her.

Kitty knew nothing about Skeat's telepathic abilities. She waited for the next thing to happen.

The moment Skeat felt Alex's touch, she kicked him hard. It was a jolt like Alex had felt only a few times before. The power of an unusually strong child, accompanied by an explosion of uncontrolled energy, sent him flying from his crouched position across the room and he slammed into the wall fifteen feet away. His eyes flashed that familiar green as he tapped into his innate abilities. He twisted with the agility of a circus performer, landing in the stance of a runner coming out of the starting blocks. He had to get her out of this place.

This time, Alex braced himself for whatever Skeat threw at him. Whatever was coming, he knew it was going to hurt. He sprinted forward and snatched her up from the floor. Her tiny body was electrified, exploding with power as she shrieked at a deafening level. She flailed wildly in Alex's arms as he clutched her tightly. She tore at his clothes and clawed at his face. Suddenly, violently, she reached out for Kitty, grasping toward her with wide green eyes, begging for help. Kitty ran to Skeat and gripped her wrist tightly, pulling her as the trio tumbled to the ground, ending with Skeat on top of Kitty. Skeat wrapped herself around Kitty, burying her face deep in the woman's hair.

CHAPTER SIX

Kitty was disoriented, lying flat on her back as the room spun around her. She felt nauseous. A foul stench of burned flesh and death hung in the air. The floor beneath her was soft, unlike the hard concrete she expected to have landed on. Blurred vision revealed a large room with walls dusted in silver sage and an equally silver-blue ceiling hovering high above. It was difficult to tell if the hard blow to her head or smoke from burned flesh had caused the opaque mist around her. Bright light streamed through a window above and to her left, revealing swirls of gray and white smoke. She squinted to see, but everything was hazy from watery eyes rejecting whatever was creating the surrounding smoke. The view to her right was further obscured by mounds of dirty, matted hair. To her left, Alex lay close and still, his face less than a foot from hers. When she turned her head toward him, tears ran down the sides of her eyes to the floor, clearing her vision slightly. His suit jacket was torn, his glasses gone, and his mouth hung open. His formerly brown eyes were the same deep emerald green as Skeat's, only his were covered in a cloudy film. They were wide open, staring through her. He looked dead. He smelled dead. A few moments later, the twitching movement of Alex's body startled her as he sprang to his feet perturbed, muttering as he stared down at her.

He hadn't meant to bring Kitty with him. The way Skeat was clinging to her on the floor, it was probably for the best. Now he had to decide. Did he try to give her some sort of explanation about what was going on and ask her for help or would it be better to entrance her and return her to the cell? He frowned at the two of them lying on the floor and considered his options. It was obvious that Skeat trusted Kitty. Alex himself felt a curious draw that made him want to trust her as well. It was also clear that this child could not stay on Earth. His mind raced with tangential thoughts. The community here wasn't equipped to deal with an energy grafter. There were a few families on Rasa who could raise her and others in the wide community off the planet he currently called home. He would make sure he found the right place before taking her back, which was yet another problem. Bringing her back in a shuttle wouldn't be possible. She might get upset and short out the whole thing. One other option would be to use the port deck back at the vineyard, but he didn't know if he wanted to risk taking her there.

Kitty started to sit up, breaking his trance, but Alex could see that her eyes were unfocused.

"Stay down. You'll thank me later." He knew how disorienting portals could be the first few times, and she hadn't been prepared for this.

"What's going on, Alex? Where are we? How did we get here?" Kitty slurred as if drunk or waking from a deep sleep.

Ignoring her question for the moment, he knelt beside her and pushed her back to the ground. "Skeat," he whispered. She made no response. He risked a light touch on her back. "Listen, Skeat, it's quiet. The voices are gone. You're home."

Skeat jerked her head up at his touch, revealing faint freckles in the clean streaks made by tears streaming down her dirty face. Alex saw a spark of recognition and was relieved that she hadn't shocked him again. She loosened her grip on Kitty's neck but didn't let go completely as she slid down Kitty's side, using her as a buffer between Alex and herself. Skeat peered over Kitty's chest at Alex. He watched as she scanned the room and slowly sat up.

"Skeat, do you know who I am?" Alex's voice remained low. She didn't answer, so he took another chance by touching her arm again.

Her head snapped toward him as she studied every detail of his face. Without warning, she jerked away and bolted upstairs.

When the girl pulled away, Kitty sat up too quickly. Her eyes rolled back, and Alex caught her arm before she collapsed to the floor. A spark of the remaining electricity from his body flashed up Kitty's arm and made her flinch.

"It's okay, she's upstairs," he said, tilting his head up and releasing his grip. He could hear Skeat rifling through the second room on the right side of the hall. It was the one that had been his when the whole family stayed here.

"What the hell is going on? How did we get here and what happened to your eyes?" Kitty asked more urgently. She was shaking.

He decided to give her a plausible explanation. He could always entrance her to forget everything later if she asked too many questions. "It's easy to conceal eye color. I wanted to be as unremarkable as possible," he said, pulling off his torn jacket and tie, revealing several darkened spots and a singed collar on his shirt. He rolled up his sleeves to reveal tattoos so realistic they could have been living, breathing things themselves.

"How we got here is a little more complicated," he said, extending his hand to help Kitty up from the floor.

She studied his casual demeanor before pulling herself off the ground, avoiding his touch. Whatever mode of travel it was, it had put her off balance.

"It's called porting," he answered the question she hadn't yet asked. "We use it to travel short distances. It can be a little disorienting if you're not prepared for it." He was glad he hadn't fixed the port blocker yet. Landing on the porch today would have been less than ideal.

"No kidding," Kitty said sarcastically. "How did you get it through the scanner with the advocate watching you like a wolf on the hunt?"

"Our technology is a notch above yours," Alex replied. He didn't want to tell her that it was an ability and not a device.

The effects of the port were slowly wearing off. Kitty scanned the room. She took a deep breath, followed by a few short sniffs. "Are we in the mountains?" She looked at Alex quizzically, feeling the need to redirect the conversation until she was fully recovered and could think straight.

"Yeah, this is the house Skeat grew up in," he replied.

"Makes sense. I used to catch her in the mountains pretty often. How'd you find it?" she asked, sitting on the far end of the sofa and rubbing her temples.

"I didn't have to find it. It's my house. I found out about Skeat and her mother when I returned here."

"Did I hear you tell Skeat it's quiet? The voices are gone? Does that mean she's a telepath? My species is telepathic, and I've never been able to communicate with her." Kitty looked at him skeptically.

"That's probably because she's wide open. I don't think she can pick apart a single communication. They all seemed to mesh and blare at her at the same time. Her mother was human, and she lived up here all her life …"

Kitty interrupted him. "You mated with a human?!" She scooted away from him as if he had a contagious disease.

"Not on purpose!" He yelled back at her.

"Oh, my god! You should be in prison."

"I was using protection. I never knew she was pregnant. She didn't even try to get in touch with me."

"So, she died giving birth to your child? No wonder you were trying to cover it up!"

"She didn't die until two years ago. She had seven years to contact me. I didn't just run away and leave her alone to deal with all of this."

"I'm sorry. I didn't mean to assume. I just see a lot of shitty parents in my line of work."

"She didn't know what I was. If she had tried to find me, I could have helped her with the child. They probably never even knew about her ability, and if they did, how were they supposed to help her? There wouldn't have been anyone to teach her how to block others out, so she hears everyone all the time." Alex felt sorry for the girl.

"Except us," Kitty noted quickly.

"We can block, so yes, except us," Alex thought that sounded like a reasonable assumption.

"Well, at least she has you now," Kitty added.

Alex averted his eyes toward the floor.

"Are you serious?" Kitty asked.

"I have a life to get back to." Alex scoffed at her.

"You have a daughter to raise!" Kitty sneered scornfully. "I suppose you'll just dump her off with the first strangers who take her into your little community, and that'll be the end of it as far as you're concerned. You'll have done your duty?"

"*I* am a stranger to her!" Alex shouted back, pointing to the ceiling. "I'm not the guy anyone should trust to raise a child. There are much better places for her than with me." He stopped talking when he saw Skeat standing on the stairs holding a drawing screen. Her expression was blank, so he wasn't sure if she had heard or understood what he and Kitty had been discussing.

"What have you got there, Skeat? Did you bring this to show me something?" Alex asked in a softer tone than he had used with Kitty. He was curious to know what it was that had changed her from a murderous rage to this unnerving calm so quickly. Did all children have this ability to shift moods in a fraction of a second, or was her behavior masking something more sinister?

Skeat held the pad out in front of her as she approached them. He sat down on the sofa about a foot away from Kitty and motioned her toward him. "Bring it over here so we can have a look at it."

Skeat approached from Kitty's side and leaned over her lap to hand Alex the screen. He placed it on the table between him and Kitty. It was set to the main screen with no images on it. Kitty put her hand on Skeat's back, causing the child to wriggle on the edge of

Kitty's knees. Apparently, Skeat didn't mind physical contact on her terms. She just didn't like it when others touched her. Kitty pulled her hand away and leaned back, giving Skeat space.

They sat in silence for a moment, with Alex and Skeat looking at each other. Alex glanced at the tablet, then back at Skeat, hoping to signal her to open the device. He was trying to build some trust by not pressing into Skeat's thoughts. She had been traumatized enough, and he didn't think that rummaging around in her head would have a positive result, no matter what he thought he could learn about her. It would be better to find some help for her than to make ineffective attempts to discover more when he wasn't going to be in her life much longer, anyway.

Skeat stretched her arm forward, keeping a wary eye on Alex, and tapped on the device. The screen was covered with hundreds of drawing files. Skeat tapped again on a file that projected the drawing into a three-dimensional object in the air above the tablet. It was a rendering of space. Alex recognized it as a familiar cluster of stars thousands of light years away that Skeat had no reason to know anything about.

"Oh, that's beautiful, Skeat!" Kitty exclaimed, accepting the child's demeanor switch at face value.

Skeat flipped through the next few drawings, all showing views of space from points outside the current galaxy.

"What a wonderful imagination you have," Kitty interjected.

Alex said nothing. He knew it wasn't imagination. These places were real. The renderings were very good. The girl had obvious artistic talent, but she must have copied the images from something. Had she seen old photos from space probes, or had she somehow pulled still images from Ida's memory data? There must be a rational explanation. As she scrolled through, the drawings became more personal. He recognized most of the planets and even some people. But these were things from a long time ago. The last drawing Skeat stopped at would require an explanation.

Kitty shot Alex a look of contempt. He could feel her eyes burning into him. Alex wanted to cut off the question he could see coming. "This is my brother and his family."

Kitty's mouth snapped shut as she looked between the rendering and Alex. There was a man, who she assumed was Alex, a tall, slender woman with thick, wavy blond hair, and a small boy on a rock by the side of a lake. The sky was a hazy blue-violet color accented by pinkish-white clouds. "He looks just like you without the beard," she said, suspicion narrowing her eyes. "You expect me to believe you have a twin?"

He really didn't want to reveal any personal information to a stranger. He also didn't want Skeat to think another family was the reason he didn't want to raise her.

"Triplets, actually. There are three of us," he answered with a hint of hesitation.

"Well, that's terrifying."

Alex gave her an uncomfortable smile as his mind flashed back through his life. It was terrifying once. Worlds that witnessed the arrival of The Three rarely existed to witness their departure. He hated himself for the things their grandfather had forced them to do in the name of expanding their realm. Erik and Mikkel had forgiven themselves, or at least found a way to live with the things they had done. Alex hadn't found that peace yet. He didn't know if he ever would.

"So, she drew these from your pictures?" Kitty asked, pulling him out of his thoughts. She was prying, and he didn't like where it was going.

"No. I've never seen any of them," Alex shrugged. He wasn't the kind of guy who took pictures. He was certain that his first thought was correct. The drawings had been made from still images, and from the composition of them, the most recent ones were at least a hundred years old. Judging by the perspective, they were probably Mikkel's. But how had Skeat come by them? As far as he knew, the last time Mikkel had been here was centuries ago.

Alex decided there were more pressing issues than wasting time reminiscing over echoes of a distant past. He placed his hand over the drawing pad and closed the hologram. Skeat sneered at him.

"Are you hungry?" he asked.

Skeat squinted up at him and furrowed her brow. Alex repeated the question and rubbed his hand over his stomach. Skeat nodded as her features relaxed slightly. Alex shifted his focus to Kitty.

"I don't think she speaks English. Her mother's first language wasn't English," he said. Gen spoke a mixture of new Spanish and a native language he had never taken the time to learn. Why acquire a new language when he could read thought waves that didn't require language? His first experience with Skeat's mind had been a deeply painful one, making Alex unsure if he wanted to try again. He didn't know what damage it could cause with him stumbling around in such a delicate mind with the finesse of a stomping troll. A language barrier might be the reason Skeat didn't acknowledge them when they spoke to her.

"Good time to think about that. What was her first language?" asked Kitty.

Alex shrugged. "Not English."

"Not helpful," Kitty shot back.

"Neither is snideness." Alex paused before adding, "It's no secret that I'm not prepared for Skeat's uniqueness."

"Ya think?"

"I need to get us some food. Could you stay for a few hours and get her into a bath while I'm gone?" Alex thought Kitty would be more useful than he had originally anticipated.

"She's nine. She's perfectly capable of washing herself," Kitty smirked.

Alex closed his eyes in a momentary pause. "Can you stay and get her to take a bath or not?" he asked more directly.

"I can try. But if you come back and smell burnt fur, you'll know what happened," Kitty said sarcastically.

Kitty got Skeat's attention and mimed washing her hair, then sniffed at Skeat and wrinkled her nose. Skeat turned her head and sniffed at herself, then slowly nodded back with a grimace on her face.

Alex stifled an amused chuckle at the pantomime. "The soap is in my shower."

"And where would that be?"

"Up the stairs, only door on the left," Alex gestured upward.

"And towels?"

"You won't need them here. I'm sure Skeat knows how to dry herself." Alex ported out of the room unexpectedly, leaving Kitty and Skeat wide-eyed.

The end point of Alex's port was a courtyard in the oldest of Vito's Italian vineyards. He had thought about the market, but he didn't know how to cook and didn't want to take the time to load the convenience system. Besides, he had to provide Vito with his report. Alex landed at the door of the villa as the sun was setting. It was impolite to port into someone's home when they weren't expecting you. Alonzo had opened the door before Alex knocked. Isa lurked in the hallway behind him.

"Where's the child?" Isa asked, peering over Alonzo's shoulder.

"Where's Vito?" Alex demanded, pushing past Alonzo and ignoring Isa.

"Alex! What happened?" Alonzo insisted on an explanation as he followed Alex down the hall to the kitchen. Isa stayed behind but followed them with her eyes.

Alex could tell that Vito was not inside the house. He went through the kitchen and out the back door, where he saw Vito talking to the estate manager.

Vito spotted Alex and started walking toward him, leaving the manager behind.

"Where's the child?" Alonzo asked, loud enough for Vito to hear.

"She's safe, but we have a bit of a problem." Alex directed his reply to Vito.

"She?" Alonzo asked.

"We do have a problem," Vito interrupted Alonzo. "I got a complaint from the facility that you disappeared with one of their trackers."

"I'll have her call in and straighten that out, but that's not the problem."

"Maybe not to you," Vito raised his eyebrows at Alex.

"She's a contractor. She doesn't have to report to them if she's done her job."

"It is a problem that I didn't hear about it from you before I got the call from them," Vito said sternly, pointing to Alex's chest. He wasn't letting Alex off the hook because of who he was. If Alex was on this planet, he had to follow their rules.

"I got here as soon as I could." Alex didn't feel he had done anything wrong. He took care of the issues he felt were important, and he didn't care if it irritated Vito.

Vito narrowed his eyes at Alex. "I don't read minds like you do, boy. Spit it out." He wasn't in the mood for guessing games and Vito didn't have the patience for Alex's disregard for procedure that his sister Vivienne had. Much as he disliked it, he had people to report to.

Alex wasn't in the mood for games, either. "I'm sorry if my death resulted in you receiving an inconvenient call."

"What do you mean, your death? Nobody said anything about killing anyone, just a disappearance." Vito wasn't sure he understood what Alex was saying to him as he looked over Alex's singed clothing.

"She's an energy grafter, Vito. I had to grab her to get her out of that pit of filth they had her locked in. She blasted me with everything she had. I had barely gotten her back to the cabin before I collapsed. Had she been any stronger, I wouldn't have made it through the port. It took me a while to recover, so I apologize for your inconvenience," Alex recounted irritably.

"What about the chaser, then? Is she all right?" Vito did not want to have to explain the death of another species at the hands of the girl. The Alliance authorities would demand that she be put down.

"She's fine. I didn't want to take her back with us, but she grabbed Skeat's arm as we walked through the port."

"Didn't she get the energy blast too?" Vito asked.

"No ... no, she didn't," Alex replied, perplexed. "When I had Skeat, she reached for the wolf. She must have at least some control, or she would have fried both of us, not just me."

"Why don't you just ask her if she can control it?" Alonzo interjected.

Alex turned his head halfway toward Alonzo, who was standing over his shoulder. "Because she doesn't speak. She can scream like a Purguran banshee, but she doesn't speak. I don't know if she's in shock, doesn't understand the language, or is just as stubborn as her mother. Kitty's known her for a few months and says she's never heard the girl speak to anyone in any language."

"Kitty?" Alonzo asked.

"The chaser," Vito snapped. "Who else would he be talking about? If you want to keep interrupting with your inane questions, you can go back to the house. Now let him finish."

Alonzo had the forlorn look of a house dog its master had kicked for no reason. He closed his mouth and stepped back.

"How does she communicate?" Vito asked.

"I'm not sure yet. She's an open telepath, which could be helpful. On the other hand, I don't know how much control she has over it. She certainly can't block anything. Being locked up with hundreds of beings with no blocking abilities may have already driven her mad. She's certainly not acting normal."

"And you know how a normal child acts?" Vito asked.

Alex scowled, having absolutely no way of knowing what normal behavior for a child was. "I think we should wait a couple of days. Let her settle in before we try to make any judgments."

Vito scratched his chin thoughtfully before speaking again. "Two days. Monitor her. You know what to do if she gets out of control."

"I understand," Alex said the words, although he had no intention of complying. He had a plan of his own.

"Ask the wolf to stay until we can figure out the best way to proceed," Vito said, as he began to walk back to the field.

"She's a contractor. I'm sure she'll stay for a price."

"Whatever it takes." Vito dismissed the comment as unimportant. "Keep me informed. I'll send my report to Rasa and the Alliance."

Alex stopped short. "I don't think this is something that needs to be evaluated by the entire community, and I don't think it's any of the Alliance's business."

Vito turned to him, "You of all people should grasp the complicated issues surrounding a potentially dangerous child. I am required to report to both authorities. It's not my decision *or yours.*"

"Which is exactly why they shouldn't be made aware of it yet. This is an entirely different situation, and if you recall, that child hadn't turned out to be dangerous either. I expected them to make a judgment based on fear, but not you."

Vito sighed. He knew Alex was not wrong. "I have to tell them something. I've already sent word that she existed, and you were going to claim her."

Alex took a few steps down the slope, closing the distance Vito had created.

"Then tell them the truth. She's traumatized from the events of the last few months and is currently nonverbal. Tell them she needs a few days before we can evaluate her."

"What do I tell them if they ask about her abilities?"

"What abilities? I don't recall mentioning any remarkable abilities." Alex threw up his hands in a gesture of denial.

"I guess you didn't," Vito agreed, tilting his head. "But, just to be clear, you are taking full responsibility."

"For now," Alex said.

"For now." Vito confirmed the response. "You have two days."

Alex nodded in agreement and held out his hand. Vito grabbed his forearm, and they clasped each other's shoulders with their free hands.

"Well, what …" Alonzo began. Vito gave him a stern look as Alonzo let his words drift into the air. After a moment's pause, he apparently decided to speak anyway, "but sir, the Regent has promised her to a family."

"*Un*-promise her. Tell them her father has taken responsibility," Vito ordered, grabbing Alex firmly by the back of his neck.

Alex swallowed hard. For now, he thought again, to reassure himself that this was only a temporary situation.

Vito let go and walked back toward the field while Alex and Alonzo turned toward the house.

"I need to take some food with me," Alex said, dismissing Alonzo as if he were a servant and not someone he had considered a friend just a few years earlier. This wasn't what he had signed up for. He was irritated and resentful of the whole situation. He didn't want this responsibility.

ALEX'S CLAIM

CHAPTER SEVEN

Alex ported into the kitchen at the cabin and set the large basket of food on the counter. Kitty sat on the sofa with Skeat on the floor in front of her so she could braid the girl's unruly mass of auburn curls. After being scrubbed clean, the child's appearance revealed light brown skin, and a freckled nose and cheeks. She was a duplicate of her mother, with Alex's distinct green eyes as the only physical feature connecting them. It was enough. He couldn't deny it any longer, not even to himself. No matter how impossible it was, she was his child. He would do whatever it took to find her a family that would raise her the way she deserved to be raised.

"I don't smell any burning flesh," Alex joked.

"We came to an agreement. She didn't electrocute me, and I didn't drown her in the bathtub," Kitty replied as she continued to braid Skeat's hair.

"You know that wouldn't be permanent, right?" Alex teased.

"I'm not an idiot. It was a joke," Kitty replied, shaking her head.

She tied off the last of the braids and motioned Skeat toward the kitchen. Skeat hopped onto one of the stools to watch Alex unpack the food. Her eyes followed each container out of the basket and onto the counter, waiting patiently. Kitty pulled plates from the cupboard and rinsed them before setting them out. Alex placed massive portions of food on all three plates and Kitty poured a glass of water for Skeat and wine from the basket for herself and Alex.

Kitty looked at the plates, then back and forth between Alex and Skeat. "I think you might be overdoing it a little."

Alex looked at the plates, then at Skeat. "You think maybe half?" He did not know how much a child of barely four stone could eat.

"Half for me, a quarter for her." Kitty snickered.

Alex reassembled the plates and pushed the smallest one with a fork and napkin in front of Skeat. Skeat gave him a questioning glance.

He pushed the plate a little closer to her. "Go ahead. Eat."

She wrinkled her nose and looked from the plate of spaghetti and roasted broccoli salad to the block of Parmigiano Reggiano next to Alex. He didn't catch on. Eyona's spaghetti was delicious. He had eaten it many times before and knew that there was nothing wrong with the food. He couldn't understand what the problem was. Kitty had seen the questioning look and knew exactly what the child wanted. She pulled a grater out of the third drawer she searched, took the block of cheese, and grated some over the pasta. Skeat looked up when it was enough, then picked up her fork and twirled a length of handmade pasta. She shoveled the oversized portion into her mouth, leaving sauce running down her chin and onto her clean shirt.

Kitty and Alex stood across from her and watched as Skeat devoured the entire plate of food while they ate at a slow pace. When the girl finished, she ran her fingers over the plate to get the last remaining drop of sauce and licked them clean. Kitty handed her a warm, damp cloth to wipe her face and hands. Skeat cleaned her mouth and fingers, then leaned against the back of the stool and yawned. It seemed the bath and warm food had done their work. The girl was exhausted. It was still late afternoon at the cabin, but Alex saw no reason to keep her awake. As tired as she looked, he estimated she would sleep through until morning. He continued to watch her head bob and pop up again as he finished his meal. When he decided she was too tired to fight him, he cautiously walked around the counter toward her. He gently lifted her from the chair. Her head fell to his chest, and she threw her arm over his shoulder. It was a very different experience than the first time he held her. Her tiny body was warm and smelled of floral soap. He carried her to her room and tucked her into her bed.

As he closed the door to Skeat's room, he had an idea to give her his sleep hood. He took it out of his bag and changed the settings from fast recovery to slow recovery with neural blocking to make sure no errant thoughts would disturb her. Placing it on the wall over the headboard, he extended it to cover the length of her torso and left the room for a second time.

When Alex descended the stairs, he could hear Kitty speaking loudly to someone on her communication device.

"What the hell do you mean you're not going to pay me?!" she shouted into the device. "Well, that's not my fault! You should have had him sign it before you sent us down!" she continued shouting as she paced.

"Fine! You don't want to pay me, I'll just bring her back since she's still your responsibility," Kitty said through gritted teeth.

Alex's heart raced at the words. He cautiously held back, waiting to hear what she said next.

She paused for a few moments, then scoffed. "That's what I thought. I'll have it back to you before your deadline."

Alex exhaled in silent relief. He should have known Kitty was bluffing, but it didn't make him resent the anxiety he felt over the statement any less.

Kitty paused again as the person on the other end spoke. "Yeah, I'm still with him. What business is that of yours?" Another few seconds of silence went by. "Could you not sound so disappointed? Just send the god-damned release and pay me my fucking money!" Kitty yelled and disconnected the call. She growled and chucked the device at the sofa.

"That sounded like it went well," Alex remarked, causing Kitty to jump.

"Shut up!" she snapped, turning quickly to face him. "It's rude to eavesdrop."

"I wasn't eavesdropping. You were yelling."

"That idiot advocate was so quick to get away from you, she forgot to have you sign the release and now she's telling me that I haven't fulfilled my contract and I'm not getting paid." Kitty stomped over to the sofa to retrieve her communicator.

"But she's sending it to you, right?" Alex asked.

"Yes, and if I can't get it back by close of business," she glanced at her timepiece, "in nine minutes, she'll void my contract."

"And you won't get paid?"

"Yeah genius. I won't get paid. This isn't the first time they've tried to pull this crap with me." Kitty looked down at her phone, checking for the release and shook her head. "This is so ridiculous. I try to do the right thing and all they want to do is screw me."

"We'll get it back to them as soon as it comes through," Alex replied calmly. As much as he disliked being verbally assaulted, he realized Kitty's anger wasn't directed at him. Calm was the best option.

"That asshole is going to wait until the last second to send it," Kitty said, checking her phone again.

"You'll get your money."

"What? Are you gonna pay me?" Kitty scoffed.

"If they don't get it to you in time, then yeah, I'll pay you," Alex offered.

"You don't even know how much it is. It was a very expensive contract," Kitty replied smugly.

"What does someone like you consider expensive?" Alex replied, not realizing how condescending the question sounded.

Kitty sneered as she scanned his face. She thought he was quickly dismissive of the amount and arrogant, which meant he must be rich. *Fuck! Why did he have to be such a smug, rich bastard?* "A million dige," she huffed.

"Dige?" Alex asked.

"Digital Credits? You live under a rock or something?"

"I've never heard them referred to like that."

"Ohhh, well, excuse me, sir. What does someone *like you* call them?" Kitty mocked.

"Well, you know *we* just call them creds," Alex needled back.

A few minutes later, Kitty's device pinged. "Thank God! Three minutes left." She opened the release and shoved an enlarged holographic document at Alex. "Here, sign this."

Alex scribbled something unrecognizable into the air over the document line. Kitty pulled it back and quickly returned the document. "Whew!" she exclaimed. "Two minutes to spare."

"It could have been closer." Alex joked.

Kitty's device alerted her. She looked down at it. "Ah, this can't be good," she said, picking up the call.

"What's the problem?" She paused. "Of course, it's his signature." She paused again. "What do you mean it doesn't match? He signed it on a fucking holograph! It's not going to be an exact match!"

Alex took the device from her. "With whom am I speaking?" He paused. "Well, you are speaking with Aleksander Johnson, and yes, I did sign the release as requested … Uh-huh. … And how exactly would you like me to prove it over a non-visual communication device, Ms. Prucell?" He paused again and rolled his eyes, becoming noticeably irritated. "Ms. Prucell," he said loudly. "Can you hold on for just a moment, please?"

Alex muted the call. Kitty began to say something, but Alex held up his finger to silence her. "What's her first name?"

"Mirium, but …" Alex silenced her again.

"Ida, display all information on Mirium Prucell of WOAC."

An immediate display of thousands of holographic documents appeared throughout the room. Kitty spun around, astonished by the sight of all the images floating around her. Alex moved too quickly for Kitty to follow, sorting through, expanding, and swiping aside mounds of information. Five seconds later, he was standing back in front of her, unmuting the call.

"Thank you for holding Ms. Prucell," he began in a calm, cold tone. "It seems we have come to a bit of an impasse about the appropriate way to resolve this situation. I have a few thoughts if you will indulge me for a moment." His silence was only momentary. "If you deny the release and decline to pay the contractor, then I would be forced to respond by reporting the issue to my Regent. That would result in a call to the Alliance authority and another one to your director, which is something I'm certain neither of us wants."

Kitty could hear that Ms. Prucell had interrupted Alex.

"Yes, Ms. Prucell, I do understand that you believe your director supports all of your decisions in these types of matters. However, if by the *slimmest* of chances, he doesn't support this *one* decision, well, would you really want to take that kind of chance?"

Alex's grin widened as Ms. Prucell spoke.

"I completely understand, Ms. Prucell, but as I was saying, tuition for two children at San Samuel Private Academy is far too expensive for you to take that type of risk, isn't it?" There was a long, silent pause. "Ms. Prucell? Are you still there?" Alex grinned at Kitty. "Ms. Winterclaw and I appreciate your decision to resolve the matter in such an amicable way. Thank you. Enjoy your evening." Alex had no sooner hung up the call and handed the device back to Kitty when it chimed with her payment.

"Remind me never to piss you off," Kitty said, absently scanning the documents hovering around her head.

"I don't think I'll have to remind you," Alex smirked. "Ida end display."

The documents melted into the air.

Kitty glanced at her device again. "Thanks."

He nodded at her. "Drink?"

"Hell yes."

Alex poured each of them a scotch and handed one to Kitty. "Where do we go from here?" he asked.

"I go home. Skeat is safe, and I have a whole list of other kids who need me."

"Any way I could interest you in twice the amount you just collected?"

"I'm not sure I want to ask what I'd have to do for that kind of money." Kitty sipped the scotch. She didn't want to stay in such close proximity to Alex, but she would be an idiot if she didn't hear him out on his offer. There weren't many opportunities for someone like her to make that sum of money. She was an independent woman, but she did owe it to her pack to listen.

"I just need you for two days."

"I'm not sleeping with you." She peered over her glass with a serious look on her face. Alex sensed a nervous energy pouring off of her, although he wasn't sure why.

"I need you for Skeat," Alex sneered back. He didn't appreciate her assumption.

"You seem to be getting on fine. Why would you need me and why only two days?" Kitty asked suspiciously.

"Because you're the only one she trusts, and I don't want her running off looking for you if you take off while she's asleep." Alex hoped that would be explanation enough.

"So, you need a babysitter."

"I need her to settle down so I can bring in someone who can figure out how to communicate with her, without her trying to blast them through the wall," Alex spat out in exasperation.

"So … you need a babysitter," Kitty repeated more slowly.

Alex sighed. "Yes. I need a babysitter."

"Okay," Kitty smiled. "See, that wasn't so hard now, was it?"

"What wasn't so hard?"

"Asking for help."

"I don't …" Alex started, but Kitty cut him off by clearing her throat. "Thank you," he decided to finish, adding a clearly reluctant smile.

"You're welcome." She smiled smugly while taking a sip of her drink. "Oh, and you'll need to go pick up some things at the town market before it closes. Unless you want to feed her spaghetti for breakfast?"

"Couldn't you do that? I don't know what kids eat."

"No, sorry." She lifted her glass as if she were toasting. "I'm on babysitting duty."

"Right," Alex answered. He despised shopping and wasn't looking forward to mingling with town locals, either. Alex downed his drink and walked toward the door.

"We also need shampoo, more soap, dish soap, and I don't have any clothes," Kitty added as Alex grabbed the doorknob.

He turned back toward her. "Anything else, princess?" he asked in a mocking tone.

"Not that I can think of, your highness." Kitty smiled back.

Alex jerked the door open and reconsidered the urge to slam it behind him when he considered that the vibration might wake Skeat. He closed it softly. This whole situation was making his nerves so raw. It had to be the reason Kitty was getting so deep under his skin. He never should have come back here. He stood on the porch for a few moments, thinking about his options. Taking the shuttle into town would be the least conspicuous choice. He didn't want to draw any undue attention by porting in. There was also an issue of not knowing the layout anymore and not having any idea where he could appear and not be seen. The ride would give him a few minutes to compose a message, anyway. There was only one person Alex could think of who had the skills to help him without judging him or making him feel guilty for giving up his child.

By the time he had arrived in town, the message had been sent. There was no unringing of the bell now. In the space of ten minutes, Alex had asked for help twice. He didn't like the feeling of needing to rely on someone else to solve his problems.

The trip into town wasn't as bad as he had remembered it. Things here had taken a dramatic turn. There were all sorts of diverse characters strolling around in the open. They certainly weren't in hiding the last time he was here, but now, they no longer had to be concerned about any human scrutiny. He had spotted a few different species of Fae, wood nymphs, elementals, and several groups of assorted shifters walking around in and out of human form. The market had a vast array of conjurers' shops and street vendors selling items that catered to a vibrant community of abilitied species. Other than a few wary stares directed toward him for being a stranger, Alex felt anonymous.

Less than an hour later, with his shopping complete, he was pulling back up the driveway to the darkened cabin. As the shuttle door opened, Alex felt the slight vibration associated with being in the presence of another turned. He felt relieved as he lifted the heavy sacks of food and other wares out of the shuttle's storage compartment. When he began climbing the porch steps, the front door opened a few inches. He pushed it with his foot, giving him enough room to enter. The second he had slipped inside, the door slammed shut and he stood, pressed against the wall, face to muzzle with Kitty's large chestnut, gold, and red wolf. She growled low, blowing her warm breath over Alex's face. Suddenly, she turned away, springing back toward the window that faced the driveway and snarled, bearing long sharp teeth. Alex collected the items he had dropped and walked toward the kitchen.

"It's all right, Kitty. He's with me," Alex said, flipping on the kitchen lights, pretending her being pressed against him hadn't bothered him.

Kitty stopped snarling and cocked her ear toward him without taking her eyes off the driveway.

"He's fine. He's not going to hurt her," Alex said, placing the bundles on the counter.

Kitty snorted toward the glass one last time before sauntering across the main room toward the kitchen. Alex watched her walk toward him while he unpacked the cold items. She was a powerful yet graceful creature in her wolf form. Her eyes glowed amber, something he thought gave her a menacing appearance he could imagine would strike fear in many. The ferocity of her wolf gave him a feeling of pride somehow. Kitty sat on the floor in front of him as he looked her over. Her wolf was huge. Much of her girth was fur, but her head reached the middle of his chest while she was sat back on her haunches. Once this graceful beast appeared, he wagered the other children of her youth had stopped tormenting her. She cocked her head at him, and he could imagine in her human form she would be standing with her hand on her hip, tapping her foot.

"I didn't know he'd be here so soon," Alex defended.

Kitty cocked her head in the other direction. He didn't need to use telepathy to understand what she was thinking.

"I didn't think about telling you he was coming."

Kitty sat up straight, pulling her shoulders back. She snorted at him and strolled into the living area, curling into a large ball of fluff on the floor.

"Fine. I'll go talk to him."

Kitty lifted her head, making a nodding gesture toward the door.

Could you at least change back to human form? Alex spoke to her telepathically. *I know you can respond to me.*

Kitty ignored him, laying her head on her paws.

"Hmph," he snorted aggressively, pushing back the sacks on the counter before heading toward the door. "Can you at least put away the food before it spoils?" Alex asked snidely. He continued past her, feeling her eyes boring holes in the back of his head. She was clearly angry at him, although he wasn't sure why. He had explained. That should have been the end of it.

CHAPTER EIGHT

Ivan was sitting alone in the dark garage when Alex turned on the lights.

"It's good to see you," Alex said. Past events had taken their toll on the man standing in front of him. Ivan appeared old and defeated. The spark was gone from his eyes.

Ivan wore a weary smile. Being in this place again seemed to cause him pain. "I seem to have agitated your friend," he replied, nodding toward the house.

With a sheepish tone, Alex admitted, "I forgot to tell her you were coming."

"Clearly," Ivan said, motioning toward the back of his torn jacket.

"You shifted into the house? No wonder she's so pissed at me." Alex could now see Kitty's behavior made a bit more sense.

"I know you've been coming here for centuries, but it is still my house, Alex. I didn't think you'd have a hellhound guarding the child." Ivan chuckled. "She's a good choice, though. Made me think twice about popping in unannounced. She was on top of me before I had a chance to phase."

"Did she bite you?" Alex asked, concerned. He'd heard the rumors that a blood wolf's bite could kill a normal vampire. He wasn't so sure it applied to them, though.

"Just a graze." Ivan didn't seem to hold the same concerns Alex did as he smirked.

Alex noticed a bit of sparkle come back to Ivan's eyes. It had been quite a while since he had seemed amused by anything. "If it's any consolation, she's already given me hell for not announcing you."

"So, are you two?" Ivan raised his eyebrow, sensing something more than an employer/employee relationship going on.

"No." Alex shook his head a bit too vehemently. He had strangely felt something for Kitty, but wouldn't admit it to himself, let alone anyone else. Gen's little surprise was enough of a bitter dose to have him swearing off women for the foreseeable future. "I hadn't even intended to bring her with us. Skeat is attached to her, though. Kitty seems to calm her down."

"Then what do you need me for?" Ivan asked, wondering if there was something Alex wasn't saying.

"Did you read Vito's report?"

"I did. He said the child was uncommunicative and unresponsive because of her current trauma and placement situation. Can't you simply read her to find her issues?" Ivan asked. Alex was a powerful telepath. Ivan didn't have any idea why he wouldn't be able to perform a task that should be simple for him.

"There was a lot he left out. I'm afraid if I dig in too hard, I might further damage her. I'm not as nuanced in the technique as you are," Alex said.

"Alex, you've been doing this for eons. Why would you think you'd cause her damage?" Ivan pressed. He could see there was more.

"She's an open telepath. She can't block anything. I've only read others who have at least some blocking abilities. Digging in is different from having an active conversation. It can be painful," Alex said hesitantly. He was taught more forceful techniques of finding the information he wanted than the nuanced ones Ivan used. Aside from reading his brothers, who he had a natural link with, he never needed to be delicate.

"I see. I also see you're still not telling me everything, are you? You asked me for help Alex. You need to trust me." Ivan didn't need to rifle through Alex's thoughts to see he was holding back.

"I do trust you!"

"Then it's time to come clean."

Alex sighed. "She's a grafter."

"*That* does make a difference." Ivan rubbed the back of his neck, taking his thinking posture.

Alex expanded on his earlier comment. "She's strong too. Much stronger than a child of nine should be. I mean, her energy is uncontrolled and off the charts. It's stronger than Mikkel's, closer to what I've seen from you."

"I doubt that. I've created entire constellations on my own. But I see your point, and since strength and abilities increase with age,

I understand your need to get her off this planet," Ivan replied. "Where do you plan on taking her?"

"Me? All I want to do is get her back to Rasa. I need your help to find someone who can take care of her; train her in a way that I can't."

"You don't want to be in her life at all?" Ivan asked.

"I didn't say that. What I said was, I know I'm not the right person to raise her or to help her. I thought you weren't here to judge me!"

"I'm not judging you," Ivan said as he leaned back against the workbench on his elbows in an open posture. "If you expect me to help you, I need to know what kind of situation you want for her. Vito said you took responsibility. I assumed you were planning on raising her, but if that's not the case, I need to know what type of involvement you plan on taking in her life so I can find the right type of placement."

"I didn't mean to snap at you. My only intention is to do the right thing for her. I've come to terms with the fact that I don't have Erik's moral sensibility or Mikkel's patience. She needs more than I am capable of giving. I don't have the temperament to parent any child, much less one with her capabilities and difficulties. Isa and Cori want me to turn her over to the Board. If I can't bring her under control in the next two days, they expect me to put her down because she's too dangerous and might upset the balance of their inter-species alliance." Alex punctuated his words by pointing outward.

"Alex, calm down. Did anyone actually say that to you?" Ivan asked in disbelief.

"No. It was implied. Vito said I knew what needed to be done if things got out of control."

"You're letting your emotions get away from you. You know they can't condemn *anyone* in the community without an open trial and a full vote. We both possess a pragmatic nature. Take your emotions out of it and let's look at this clearly."

"It *is* emotional! They have their own laws here. They even insinuated that I intentionally fathered a child with a human, which is grievously offensive! I'm enraged that anyone would think I would deliberately place an innocent at risk and then abandon them without a second thought."

Ivan closed his eyes for a second. He needed to control the tone of the conversation. "Every planet has their own laws. Community members need to live and interact with other inhabitants of the places they choose. The only difference here is that outside of the Alliance representatives, most species of this world don't know anything about the other residents of The Everything. The old ones are trying to maintain their way of life, and Skcat could be a threat to that existence. I'm sure they are only trying to manipulate you into getting her away before Rasans are exposed to the general population."

Alex scoffed. "That's what I'm trying to do! But she's been here for over nine years, and no one has noticed her. Now they expect me to have her ready to go in two days. She's a scared child. She doesn't trust me, and I don't know if I can shuttle her out of here. I asked you for help because you don't need a shuttle or a physical port. You can shift."

"She's certainly been noticed now. The WOAC has noticed her and now they suspect the old ones might be hiding things from them the Alliance doesn't know about. They don't realize the Alliance already knows," Ivan explained.

"But the old ones don't have any higher abilities. They were turned from humans," Alex argued.

"The general population doesn't know that. They could turn on the old ones and at that point the old ones' only options would be to leave or defend themselves violently, and neither the community nor the Alliance would condone that behavior. You need to look at the bigger picture," Ivan concluded.

"No. They have a third option." Alex shook his head and paced. His eyes shifted as dark thoughts invaded his mind. "They're not going to let her go. The Board is going to give her to the Alliance. They're going to sacrifice her to show the other species she's some kind of mutation and they will let them kill her to keep the peace."

"They're part of the community. They wouldn't do that," Ivan said, defending the old ones.

Alex rubbed his head. His darker thoughts were overtaking his rational mind. "They may be turned, but they have never been part of the community. Just because they share our link doesn't mean they are part of us. Their allegiance is to the Alliance! All of them stayed behind and rejected our ways when we left. They don't embrace our technology and they don't see themselves as Rasans. They could sever ties with us and go back to being the animals they were before. You know they still call themselves vampires, don't you? It's what they want to be. This is just the excuse they need," Alex said, speculating about their motives.

"That's conjecture, Alex. You're letting your imagination get away from you. No one would have pressured you into laying claim to her if that was their plan. They would have left her where she was and let the Alliance act against her. It seems to me their intent was to hide her existence." This was not the direction Ivan wanted this conversation to take.

"The Board didn't encourage me to claim her. Vito did. The day he called me to see him, Isa and Cori showed up and they didn't appear supportive of the idea. When I went to tell Vito what happened when I claimed her, Alonzo said that the Regent had already promised her to a family. Less than a day and they already had her placed? They didn't even know what her abilities were. Vito gave me two days to have her ready for assessment. I don't think he would be involved, but something doesn't seem right here," Alex replied, with deepening paranoia as his movements became more agitated.

"Alex, you can't always look at the worst scenario. Not everything is a conspiracy," Ivan said, trying to reel him back.

"Do you think I like thinking those things?" Alex stepped closer to Ivan. "I hate the way those thoughts come to me. From childhood, my mind was shaped to think that way. I was trained to always prepare for the worst outcome."

"That was a long time ago," Ivan pointed out.

"Not long enough. Let me ask you, Ivan, when you walk into a crowded room and meet new people, what are your first thoughts? Do you think about the room being beautifully decorated, the nice atmosphere? Do you wonder about what kind of family life or work the person you are meeting has?"

"I think that's fairly accurate," Ivan answered.

"Well, when I walk into the same room, my first thought is to assess all the egress points. I need to know which are closest, which are easiest to access. I see which items I could best use to defend myself or where an attack would be likely to come from. When I meet a new person, I initially assess them for weaknesses. I need to know exactly how I can defeat everyone in the room and what the response would be if the assembly was under siege. I instantaneously gauge whether an individual is going to be useful to me in any given scenario. Even my work keeps me constantly assessing my skills so I can teach the newly turned how to defend themselves. My grandfather ensured I would be a perfect warrior, a killing machine. It's not something that simply goes away because I don't like my view of the world."

Ivan stared at him for a moment. "No. It isn't something that goes away. It's something that you have to work at. You can't change the way you look at the world if you keep repeating the same behavior. If you don't like the way you see things, you need to find another view. Take responsibility for yourself and stop using what happened to you in the past as an excuse not to change."

Ivan's words stung him. Alex sneered. "It's not as simple as that. How could you possibly understand what it takes to change your nature?" he asked heatedly.

Ivan laughed at him. "Are you serious? Those things were never in your nature. Look at yourself. Anyone can see you loathe the things you've done. I killed for centuries because I *enjoyed* it. I was far worse off than you."

Ivan's statement shocked him. Alex had never associated Ivan with those things, although he should have. The archives were full of documentation of their species' evolution. He dropped his head in resignation. "How did you change?"

"Circumstance. Our survival was in peril. We were being hunted for the things we were doing, and it was clear that change was necessary. I had been turned as an act of revenge and I was angry for a very long time. Once I laid down that anger, I was able to move beyond it and see what needed to be done. I'm not going to tell you it was easy. It was very hard and at times I wasn't always sure I could do it." Ivan took a deep breath and stood straight. "We're getting off topic. Let me go speak with Vito. I'll know if they're being truthful, and I can scan the child when I come back."

Alex nodded.

"You should go apologize to the wolf," Ivan added before shifting away.

Alex rolled his eyes and sighed. He knew he owed Kitty an apology.

Alex slid down the wall to sit on the floor of the garage. The turn had connected him to the rest of the community, but it didn't take away the painful memories of his past. If anything, it amplified his protectiveness toward those closest to him. He had always understood threats from outside. They were obvious. Before the turn, he had also needed to assess threats from within. But could there really be any threats from within this community, or was he conjuring them up, like Ivan pointed out, simply because he was looking for them? Maybe he hadn't evolved as much as he thought. Maybe he was so obsessed with finding an enemy to fight he was seeing things that weren't there. If there was no enemy, did he even have a purpose? Sitting by himself wasn't getting him anywhere. It was only delaying the inevitability of facing Kitty's wrath. He pushed himself off the floor and headed toward the house.

"Kitty?" He said, opening the door slowly. He half-expected to dodge something being thrown at him. Silence was all that permeated the room as he closed the door.

Kitty was in the kitchen, in human form, and dressed in the clothes he had purchased for her from the market. Alex approached her slowly.

"I'm sorry you felt Ivan was a threat." Alex's attempt at an apology was clumsy.

"You're sorry I felt threatened by someone unexpectedly appearing in your house while I was responsible for watching your daughter?" Kitty asked cynically.

"Yeah, that's what I said," Alex reiterated his point.

"Being a caretaker is a little different from being a guard. He scared the shit out of me when he appeared out of nowhere in the middle of the living room!" Kitty raised her voice.

"Ivan's not a threat!" Alex yelled back.

"How the hell was I supposed to know that?!" Kitty yelled even louder.

"Shhh!"

"Did you just shush me?" Kitty whisper-screamed.

"You're going to wake her up!" Alex whisper-screamed back through gritted teeth.

Fuck you, asshole! She shouted into his mind.

Oh, that's mature, Alex countered.

"Look at you, using words you don't understand," Kitty retorted snidely.

"What in all hells is that supposed to mean?"

"You can't even put together an apology without making it sound like I'm at fault for having feelings. Do you think maybe it wouldn't have happened at all if you hadn't withheld important information?"

"I'm sorry you feel that way," Alex replied.

"There it is again! You're sorry I have feelings. Do you have any idea what an apology is?" Kitty asked.

"I just apologized to you! What do you expect, personalized letterhead and an embossed seal?" Alex asked, his voice dripping with sarcasm.

"No, what I expect is a genuine apology. Not words placating me while taking no responsibility for your own actions. I expect an apology where *you*," Kitty poked him in the chest, "take responsibility for *your* actions. Something like I'm sorry *I* didn't tell you that Ivan was coming. Or if that's too hard, how about I'm sorry Ivan's unexpected appearance scared you? *I* should have told you he was coming." Kitty pointed at him, bouncing her finger. "Do you see the difference there? Saying words denoting *your* regret at causing someone else discomfort. That … is … an apology,"

Kitty stared at him with her hands splayed and her mouth open.

Alex was stunned. He hadn't been spoken to in that way since he was a child. He instinctively went on the offensive. "Why should I have regretted the way you reacted because you were uncomfortable? Reaction to any situation is the only thing we have one hundred percent control over. If you regret your reaction, it's your own fault."

Kitty scoffed in exasperation. "You don't owe me an apology for *my* reaction, you idiot! You owe me an apology for withholding information, creating a situation that forced me to react at all. I bit your friend because I didn't expect to find him in the house while I was responsible for your child. Did you think I wouldn't protect her?"

"Of course, I believed you would protect her. I wouldn't have left you here with her if I didn't." Alex really needed to figure out what she wanted from him. She made him so angry in one second and upset that he had offended her in the next. All he wanted was to get through the next couple of days.

"Were you testing me?" Kitty wondered if Alex had set her up for a confrontation with Ivan.

"No. I didn't think he'd be here before I got back."

"But there was a possibility he could have," Kitty said.

"I didn't think so when I messaged him. He was coming from pretty far away."

"You people can - what did you call it, port? What does distance matter?"

"It doesn't, but I still didn't think he'd come inside of an hour. I told him Skeat was sleeping."

"But you obviously didn't let him know you weren't here, and that I was," Kitty stated emphatically. "Are you saying there isn't any part of that situation you could have prevented?" Kitty was irritated. She hoped she was leading him to understand her point of view.

Alex thought for a second. "I regret not telling you Ivan was coming beforehand." The statement came in a way someone would blurt out a quiz answer that had popped into their mind.

"Thank you," Kitty said sharply. That was as much of an apology as she was going to get, and she was tired of explaining. She shook her head, walking toward the front door. When she pulled it open, she sniffed at the air.

"Where is he?" Kitty asked.

"He had to run an errand. He'll be back soon. You're not going to bite him again, are you?" Alex asked, smirking at her.

Kitty looked back over her shoulder, scowling at him. "No!" she exclaimed. Her scowl slid into a grin. "Why? Are you afraid he's going to turn into one of us?"

The smirk fell off his face. "What?! Could that happen?" Alex was horrified. He hadn't even considered the ramifications of a blood wolf's bite outside of death.

Kitty laughed and closed the door, leaning against it. "No, you idiot. We're born this way. *Our* bite doesn't change people."

Alex's body slumped with relief. "That wasn't funny."

"It was. Plus, you deserved it." Kitty pushed herself away from the door. She tilted her head, examining his posture intently. "You don't seem to know very much about the rest of us. All the information that has come out in the last few centuries about species that live here, and you don't seem to have any idea. Where'd you say you were from?"

"I didn't," Alex answered, lifting one eyebrow.

She moved closer to him. "Hm. I've heard rumors, you know. Stories were there used to be a huge population of vampires and then one day, poof, ninety percent of you were gone. Just disappeared. Some say you found a secret planet on the other side of the universe. But those are just stories, right?"

Alex didn't miss a beat. He sat back, leaning against the sofa with his arms outstretched across the cushions. "Or it could be that our blood supply was poisoned, wiping out everyone who hadn't converted to synthetic blood or didn't have their own personal stash."

"That's what you're going with? Your species doesn't drink blood anymore. They haven't for centuries."

"Did you ever consider something like that was what prompted us to find a cure?" Alex asked, feeling on his game.

"You'd think that would have been something the rest of us would have heard about, wouldn't you?" Kitty cocked her head the other way. Her suspicions were growing. Something about Alex wasn't right. She hadn't met many vampires other than him, Skeat, and the guy in the garage in person, but she just felt like something was off.

Alex wasn't about to confirm anything, although sharing the truth with her was exactly what he wanted to do. He thought about blurting it all out to her, giving the Board something else to focus on besides Skeat. He might stand a better chance of getting the child home safely by creating a chaotic situation. There was still plenty of time to think about making that move. He would wait until he had spoken with Ivan before taking such a bold step.

"Believe what you want to. I wasn't turned back then, so I don't know what to tell you." He hoped she would drop the subject. Presenting an alternate theory was one thing. He wouldn't out-and-out lie to her if she pinned him down.

A knock on the door saved him from further explanation.

CHAPTER NINE

"You're right about one thing, Ivan," Isa said, turning away from the window. "We don't think he should influence this girl."

"Speak for yourself, Isa," Vito protested.

"Why?" Ivan asked.

Isa sighed. "He's impetuous, erratic, and generally unstable. He has very loose morals and treats women like they are objects created for his personal use and you want to have him in charge of a female child. Most importantly, he doesn't want to be responsible for her."

Vito approached Isa to defend his position. "Personally, I think the responsibility is exactly what he needs. He has no reason to act any differently than he does. The child will stabilize him."

Ivan shook his head. "Vito, while I see your point, this girl has had far too much instability in her life to use her as an experiment to modify behavior in Alex that you find unsavory."

"Exactly my point!" Isa emphasized.

"And you, Isa, also do not have any right to remove a child from a parent because you don't like their past choices. He hasn't done anything to prove he wouldn't be a responsible parent," Ivan said, admonishing her prejudice against Alex.

"We don't think he can provide a stable environment! The Board's only concern is the welfare of the child," Isa insisted.

"He doesn't trust that you have the child's best interest at heart. It's true that Alex doesn't feel he can raise Skeat on his own, but he wants to remain involved in her life." Ivan explained.

"The last day hasn't given him enough encouragement to try?" Vito asked.

"Well, we could arrange with the family we've chosen to let him have visitation, but only if he doesn't take her off planet. We would need to monitor their interaction," Isa said, conceding her firm stance.

"Isa, he doesn't want her raised here. He wants her taken back to Rasa and, honestly, I feel that's the best place for her. We have many more resources tailored to her abilities there." Ivan expressed Alex's wishes.

"What abilities, Ivan?" Isa snapped back at him as she saw Vito's face go pale. "Vito? What abilities?"

Ivan hadn't realized that Vito hadn't told Isa. She had been his greatest confidant for the last several centuries. "We don't know yet," Ivan said as the lie created a bitter taste in his mouth. "With Alex's background, she could have any number of abilities manifest as she grows. Rasa is prepared for them. You aren't."

"She's a *Terran* vampire, Ivan. We're concerned she won't be raised with proper values, and we have the right to monitor her progress. If something manifests that we can't deal with, you'll be our first call," Isa said.

"And Alex has the right to take her home with him," Vito said, clenching his fist.

"You're concerned about our values? You still refer to yourselves as vampires. That was a slur given to our species because of our bloodlust and beastly behavior." Ivan knew as soon as he made the statement, he shouldn't have taken such a low shot at them. They were only looking out for the girl.

Isa stepped up aggressively to him. "And you have lost perspective on your past. We keep the marque to remind us of what we have evolved from. We live simple lives here without gallivanting through The Everything, blending our blood lines with other species. It is unnecessary for us to advance beyond our peers on Earth. We are content with what we have." Vito gasped at Isa's boldness.

"You mean, like me?" Ivan glared at her. Despite not detecting any deceit, he couldn't let Isa's brazen statements go unchallenged. Grace hadn't been some stray mutt that distorted their species' purity.

Isa swallowed hard and backed down. She had gone too far. "No, Ivan. I didn't mean it like that," she said weakly, shaking her head.

Ivan stepped toward her, closing the gap between them to a few inches. "If it wasn't for me, you wouldn't have evolved at all. You'd still be killing each other's clans and murdering humans for food. Or maybe we would all have been hunted into extinction." Ivan's tone was low and menacing. Then his face softened, and his voice lowered to a whisper. "And if it hadn't been for Grace, you wouldn't have any of this peace you cherish so much." He motioned his hand across the room inattentively.

Isa lowered her eyes to the floor. She could no longer look at him. Ivan had given up so much to give them the right to live the way they wanted.

"No one is debating that point," Vito said, glancing at Isa. "You mentioned you would help with the child when Alex takes her back to Rasa?" Vito framed it as a question, trying to remove discomfort from the room. "What do you think of her?"

"I haven't met her yet, but you have my word that I will make sure she is properly cared for," Ivan answered, moving his eyes away from Isa toward Vito.

"Then it's settled," Vito said, "Isa? The matter is settled, correct?"

Isa hesitated to look at Vito. She begrudgingly spoke. "It seems so."

"Good. And how long before you expect to return to Rasa?" Vito questioned.

"A few days, I think. I'll let you know if we require more time," Ivan replied.

"Please keep us informed of your progress," Isa added, raising her eyes to meet Ivan's. They were filled with worry as well as guilt for what she had previously said. "We are truly concerned for her well-being."

"About that ..." Ivan turned toward Vito.

"Yes?"

"Alex said you told him to kill her if things got out of control." Ivan pressed in on Vito's thoughts, awaiting an answer.

"Whoa now!" Vito's hands flailed in the air as he quickly retreated. "I said *no* such a thing. I said he knew what to do, meaning to *stake* her until she could be properly subdued. You know that's how we handle things here. You implemented that policy when you were Regent!" Vito shook his head, clearly offended. "I would never ask him to kill anyone, let alone his own child. What kind of monster do you think I am?!" Vito vehemently defended himself.

It was clear to Ivan that Alex, being unfamiliar with local policy, had misinterpreted the conversation. "I'm sorry, Vito. I had to ask."

The accusation chafed Vito. "His paranoia is out of control."

"I see that," Ivan said.

~~~~

Alex sped to the door, pulling it open before Kitty realized he had moved. Ivan leaned in and scanned the room before stepping through.

"Ivan, you don't need to knock," Alex said, shaking his head.

"I thought it a better option this time." Ivan winked. He approached Kitty, extending his hand. "No hard feelings, I hope. You must be Kitty."

Kitty returned his gaze with a bashful glance. "I am so sorry. If I'd have known you were coming, I wouldn't have attacked you."

Ivan took her hands in his. "No, I never should have popped in the way I did. I haven't been to this house in centuries, and it was rude of me to assume no one else would be here. I was glad to see the child being so well protected."

"Well, I appreciate you saying that. I still feel awful about the whole thing. At least let me fix your jacket," Kitty said, apologizing. She reached toward the torn flap hanging at Ivan's side.

He slid off the garment, holding it out to her. "That would be wonderful. Thank you."
~~~~

Kitty took the jacket from Ivan, examining it closely. "Hmm …
I thought this hole was bigger."

"I guess not," Ivan shrugged. All Rasan clothing was infused
with a minute amount of self-mending nanites. Even though the tear
would be completely gone in a day or two, he preferred for Kitty to
be in another part of the house while he talked to Alex.

Kitty turned to Alex. "Do you have a sewing kit?"

Alex shrugged.

"Top of the stairs, turn right. Last room at the end of the hall.
Alex's mother keeps an odds and ends basket in her office," Ivan
replied, smiling.

"Oh, you know Alex's mother?" Kitty was thrown off by Ivan's
response.

"I certainly hope so. She's my mate."

Kitty glared at Alex and pointed at Ivan. "This is your father?"

Ivan chuckled. "No. I met his mother after they were born."

"So, this is *your* house," Kitty said, looking around.

"It's a family home, but it's been some time since I've been here.
It's got more expensive lipstick, but the bones are still the same."
Ivan scanned the room with a wistful grin.

"Now I feel even worse. I bit you in your own house."

"Don't even think about it. If you fix my jacket, we'll call it
even."

"I'll have it done before you know it." Kitty nodded, moving
toward the stairs.

Once she was out of sight, Ivan reconsidered his position. He
couldn't be sure Kitty wouldn't be able to hear them from upstairs.
He turned to Alex. "We should go for a walk."

A while later, Alex stood atop an outcropping of rock with his back toward a thousand-foot drop. It was dark, and the air was damp. The chill wind steadily blew, carrying the final scents of fall. A few yards in front of him, Ivan leaned against the smooth cool face of sheared off stone jutting upward aside the hiking path, wishing he had kept his jacket. They had already been arguing for an hour.

"If I were Vaeweth and said it, you wouldn't think it was such a preposterous idea," Alex said, annoyed that Ivan wasn't taking him seriously.

"If you were Vaeweth, you'd never suggest something so outlandish unless you had all the facts. There isn't always an enemy, Alex."

Alex exhaled a frustrated sigh. "I don't think it's so outlandish to suggest they want to take her and turn her over to the Alliance in order to appease them. I don't think it's so outlandish to think they want to appear meeker than they are to keep the peace here. And I don't think it's so outlandish for them to want to eliminate anyone who appears threatening, even if she is a child!"

Ivan pressed his head back into the rock. "The only thing they are concerned about is how dangerous she could become if she was raised under the influence of someone as paranoid as you are acting right now." He emphasized his words, lifting his head off the rock and locking eyes with Alex.

"It's not paranoia when I know they're withholding something! Vito all but escorted me to go get her and the Board immediately wanted me to hand her over. They want her for a reason, Ivan. There is always a reason." Alex began to pace, perilously close to the cliff edge.

"Look at the situation from their perspective. Hell, look at the way you're behaving right now. They want to protect her, just like you do. They want someone else to raise her, just like you do. The only difference is, they want to be able to monitor her. They are worried about how negative influences could affect her as she gets older, and her power grows."

"And what? They think I'm the negative influence?" Alex asked, pointing to himself.

"Yes," Ivan answered, nodding.

"Ridiculous!" Alex huffed.

"Is it? What would your mother say about the way you're acting?"

Alex's face contorted into a painful scowl. "If my mother was here right now, I wouldn't have a child to be discussing! I never would have had a reason to come here a decade ago at all!" he screamed at Ivan.

Ivan slid his hands into his front pockets, impassively staring at Alex. "That didn't answer the question," he finally said.

Alex deflated. He knew exactly what the answer was. It was something she had said to him hundreds of thousands of times. "She would think I was manifesting my own daemons into existence."

"And?" Ivan probed for the rest of it.

"You can't judge someone's intent solely by their actions," Alex finished.

"So, instead of judging Isa and Vito for what they may or may not have said, and jumping to conclusions, why didn't you just ask them what their intentions were?"

Alex shrugged.

"Because you didn't care before you went to get her?"

Alex stood looking at his feet.

"You said you didn't want to go get her in the first place. All you wanted to do yesterday was dump her off with the Board and go back to your life. They still want her and now you're mad about it. What changed? Is all this because you're feeling guilty for not wanting her?"

Alex grimaced and turned to face the chasm below. He spoke to Ivan over his shoulder. "I didn't expect her to be so fragile. She's so sad and scared. How can they expect me to hand her over and walk away?"

Ivan laid his head back against the rock again. "You're the parent here. You get to decide what happens with her."

"I can't teach her how to be a good person, Ivan. I can't teach her to trust people. Hells, I can't even teach her how to control her abilities. I'm useless to her." Alex looked upward, surveying the sky for an answer that would never come.

"Now you're just feeling sorry for yourself. Instead of listing all the things you can't do for her, maybe it's time to think of some things you can do for her."

"The first thing I can do for her is take her back to Rasa. Get her away from this place and these people," Alex said bitterly.

"There's nothing wrong with this place or these people. You're seeking a reason to justify being angry at them instead of yourself. Honestly Alex, you don't need to be angry at anyone. Now, why do you think Rasa is a better place for her?"

Alex knew Ivan was right, and it irritated him. He directed his gaze downward, staring through the abyss into the river below, and bit at his lip while Ivan waited patiently for a response. It was several moments before Alex spoke again.

"I think Rasa is a better place for her because there are more resources for her there. The overall feeling of the planet is peaceful, quiet, and she doesn't have to be reminded every day that everyone that loved her is dead," he replied calmly.

"And maybe because it's a place where you can watch over her and make sure she's safe?"

Alex nodded as he spoke. "I do want to make sure she's safe."

"Then that's what you need to tell the Board," Ivan said as an end to the matter. "C'mon, it's freezing out here. Let's go back to the cabin."

Alex turned to face Ivan, nodding in agreement. Ivan stepped toward him, placing his hand on Alex's shoulder, and shifted them out.

When they appeared back at the cabin, they were standing in the middle of the main room. Ivan's repaired jacket was lying across the arm of his favorite lounge chair. Kitty was asleep on the sofa. She stirred, sniffed at the air, and dropped her head back onto the pillow. The sight made Ivan chuckle to himself. There would be no second attack today.

Ivan twisted his head, cracking his neck. "I haven't showered for a couple of days. I should clean up and shave before Skeat wakes up."

"Yeah, and I should probably change out of this suit."

"I wasn't going to say anything." Ivan frowned, surveying the outfit. "It is a very odd look for you."

"It's been an odd day."

The men headed upstairs. At the top of the steps, they both turned left toward the primary bedroom, bumping shoulders. Ivan grimaced at Alex.

"I … um … I'll just grab my bag," Alex stammered, awkwardly sliding past Ivan.

Ivan followed him into the room, watching Alex stuff his belongings back into the pack before backing into the hall, pulling the door shut.

Alex headed toward his old room before remembering that was where Skeat was sleeping. The room across the hall was Mikkel's, and it was as good as any. The door was already open, so he slipped in. He changed into his standard outfit of black tactical pants and a black t-shirt with green stitching around the collar band. The familiarity of his own clothing made him feel more comfortable, more like himself. He sat on the bed, leaning back against the headboard. There was a lot for him to think about tactically, without emotion, and that was exactly the type of thinking he had always been capable of doing in these clothes, which may or may not have been a good thing.

When he pressed his head back against the headboard, something caught his eye on the bookcase on the opposing wall. He squinted and leaned forward. On the topmost shelf, two small white discs sat on the edge like shirt buttons, only thinner. He scrutinized them for a moment. Suddenly, his eyes widened as his brain grasped what they were. He jumped off the bed, racing to Skeat's room. He searched frantically for the pants she had on when he met her in that little cell at the orphanage. The clothes weren't in her room. Remembering the pungent odor of her pressed into the corner with her hand tightly clasped around something, he sniffed at the air. Following the odor, he moved down the hall to the bathroom. Alex reached into the empty clothes bin simultaneously noticing the old laundry chute on the wall. Kitty must have thrown them down to distance herself from the stench.

Alex ported himself down to the old laundry room behind the kitchen. On the floor in front of him were Skeat's pants and shirt. He snatched the pants off the floor and pulled out the pockets. They were empty. He turned them upside down and shook them hard. Across the room, he heard the ting of something small and light hitting the tile floor. Jerking his head toward the sound, he caught a glint of moonlight brush over something shiny rolling toward the drain. He dove at it, capturing it between two fingers a fraction of a second before it would have been gone forever. Holding it up to his face showed it to be exactly what he believed it was. It was a white image disc with a small green dot at the center. Placing it in his palm, he used his other hand to make a circular motion over it. Nothing happened. It was dead.

Alex tapped his ring, activating his tactical gear. He reached up, feeling a tiny depression on the side of his visor, and pressed the disc against it. Thin wire-like strands stretched out to encase the disc, absorbing it into the side of the visor. Alex used his thoughts to charge it and view the contents. Skeat's drawings came to life in images dancing before his eyes. Everything she had drawn plus hundreds more. Both still pictures and video files filled the disc. Family outings, vacations, festivals, and celebrations of all types opened.

There were images of people he knew and many he didn't. Planets Mikkel had visited in his early travels moved across. The oldest few hundred images on the disc were of this very cabin. Ivan, Alex, and his brothers took up a majority of the section. Happy memories of Erik and Ivan repairing a salvaged car slipped past. The last twenty or so were of his mother, Ami, and Violet on the back deck before they found Rasa. They looked like they had been taken from the kitchen through the open doors as the women sat around a fire pit drinking wine. That was the end of them.

Half of the best memories of Mikkel's lifetime had spilled out. Such precious reminders were put up on a shelf to be forgotten until a little girl found them. How had the disc gotten back here to be set upon its shelf grave? The newest pictures were more than a century old. Had Mikkel been coming back here randomly the whole time? He must have been. There was no other way for the disc to have gotten here and been so carefully placed. Alex raised his hand to the side of the visor, commanding threads to uncoil and deposit the disc into his palm. He tapped his ring again, deactivating his gear. He glided silently through the kitchen, slipping the memories into his front pocket.

As he passed Kitty, he could hear a gentle gurgling growl that could pass for purring emanating from her throat. It wasn't loud enough for anyone to mistake for snoring, although the sound did have an animalistic quality. He continued past her toward the stairs. As he placed his foot on the bottom step, she stirred, burying her face deep into the pillow and whimpering quietly while her breathing rate increased.

"Everyone has their own daemons," he muttered to himself, continuing up the staircase to Mikkel's room.

He was curious to see what was on the other discs. He picked up the first one with a yellow dot and circled his hand over the top. Club diagrams and pictures of construction hovered over his palm. Alex scanned through them quickly. Different planets, different clubs, inventories, construction orders, nothing of interest to him, or anyone else he would imagine. The other one also had a yellow dot revealing more of the same. The only one that had anything significant on it was the one in his pocket.

Alex flipped the disc over in his hand, wondering when Mikkel had left it at the cabin. He had no idea his brother was still visiting this place, but Mikkel had been here at least once this century. A few of the social clubs on the second disc were only a few decades old. Alex placed the yellow dotted discs back on the shelf. It seemed coming here was something his brother didn't want to share. Fair enough, Alex thought. He had things of his own he didn't want to share with his brothers either; his current situation being one of them.

At least now he knew where the drawings had come from. It was ironic to think Skeat could have used her ability to recharge the drained disc at any time if she had known how.

Alex sighed, flopping backward onto the bed. He had had no time to process the events of the day. What had he been thinking accusing the Board and, in extension, the Alliance of such ludicrous things? He *knew* these people. When he was here the last time, he had worked with them for an entire year. He interacted superficially with leaders of nearly every clan, pack, and coven they had. They weren't scheming violent people. He wholeheartedly wished his mind didn't constantly jump to the worst plausible conclusions. He desperately needed to figure out a way to change that. Those thoughts led to nothing but anxiety and suspicion of those closest to him. Maybe that was why he plowed his way through insignificant relationships with women. He couldn't let himself trust any of them. Gen included, it would seem. Had he sabotaged that himself, too? Maybe she couldn't trust him to be there for her because he wouldn't trust her. It was a vicious and infinite loop he had trapped himself in.

Before he recognized what was happening, he had drifted off with his unconscious mind forcibly seized in a swirl of what ifs and unexplained whys.

CHAPTER TEN

The dull thud of something heavy crashing to the floor, followed by clattering noises emanating from somewhere close by, startled Alex awake. He jumped to his feet, jerking open his bedroom door to land in an empty hallway. Another clang of something metal hitting hard against something solid directed him toward Skeat's room. He threw the door open to see Skeat frantically tearing through a pile of clothes on the floor. When she saw him standing in the doorway, she scampered up the overturned dresser, taking on a defensive posture.

Ivan quickly came to stand behind Alex, who was in the doorway. Skeat shrieked and charged toward the men with her hands stretched out in front of her. Alex deftly sidestepped the girl to avoid her painful touch. Ivan stood his ground without fear. Skeat's hands landed on his stomach, emanating sparks as her energy charge met Ivan's torso. She had expected him to fly backward and writhe with pain, but he simply absorbed the bolt without moving. Confused by the reaction, she drew back, balling her hands into tiny fists. She pounded them into Ivan's stomach, sending out thin streams of electricity with an angry screech. An errant spark flew away, hitting the wall in front of a concerned and confused Kitty running up the stairs.

Ivan again surprised the child by creating an energy bubble around them that filled the hall to deflect any additional unaimed charges getting loose. Skeat stumbled back a step, terrified by the field. She growled and pounded the barrier with her fists. When the membrane didn't give way, she continued kicking, pounding, and screaming. Ivan sat on the floor, leaning against the wall created by the field, and let her throw her fit. When she had become nearly exhausted, she slammed her body into the side, bouncing back and landing hard on the floor. The action spurred Kitty to lunge forward.

"Stop it! You're hurting her!" Kitty screamed.

Alex quickly ported from the bedroom doorway on the other side of the dome, placing himself between it and Kitty. He grabbed her wrists, driving her back against the wall, pinning her in place.

"Kitty, no. That field will hurt you," Alex said, as calmly as he could, feeling heat emanating from Kitty's body.

"It's hurting her!" Kitty screamed back, elevating her temperature even further.

"No! It isn't!" Alex yelled back at her. "It can't hurt her."

Kitty struggled against Alex's grip. He grabbed her face, forcing her to focus on him. "It can't hurt her," he repeated softly. "It can't."

Skeat crawled back to the side of the boundary and leaned against it, slapping it with her palm. Tears trickled down her cheeks and snot ran out of her nose. The girl slumped down onto the floor, crying silently, and stared at Ivan with her back pushed against the energy field. The pungent scent of fear and sour tones of despair made their way toward Ivan inside the bubble.

"See," Alex said, looking over his shoulder, "she's fine. It was just a tantrum." He let go of Kitty's wrist and took a step back. A shiver raced down his spine when he stepped away from her warmth.

Kitty grimaced at Ivan. "How is he doing that?" Her head snapped back at Alex. "What the hell are you people?"

Alex glanced back at Ivan, who nodded at him. "I'll explain it to you downstairs." Alex placed his hand on the small of Kitty's back and motioned her to go ahead of him.

"I'm not leaving her here alone with him!" Kitty pointed at Ivan and jerked away from Alex.

"This isn't your business, Kitty!" Alex snapped at her.

She shoved him away. "You made this my business when you asked me to stay!" she yelled back at him.

Ivan cleared his throat, and the pair spun to look at him. "Neither of you are helping," he said, keeping his voice low. "Please. Go downstairs."

Kitty clenched her jaw and snarled. Understanding there was little else she could do, she stomped down the stairs, with Alex following close behind.

Ivan let his eyes land on Skeat and sighed. He did not know how to get her talking or ease her fears, but he did know how to get her attention. He sat with his hands in his lap, forming a cup, rubbing them in a slow, circular motion. A small ball of light formed. He continued his motion until the light reached the size of a baseball. He removed his top hand. Skeat watched as the ball hovered over his palm. Ivan began tossing it from one hand to the other as the girl's eyes followed. He eased the ball to rest in a position slightly above the floor and rolled it toward Skeat, so it stopped within her arm's reach.

She tilted her head to look under it, perplexed that it wasn't touching the floor. With caution, she extended her hand towards it, gently prodding it with her finger, all while keeping a watchful eye on Ivan over the ball. She snatched her hand back, watching it roll a few inches backward while continuing to hover. Skeat's eyes quickly went to her fingertip, then back to the ball.

Ivan extended his hand, motioning forward. The ball moved closer to Skeat, and she scampered to sit up, looking between him and the ball. He then moved his hand from side to side, lulling the ball to follow his motion.

Skeat rubbed her eyes and snotty nose with the sleeve of her pajama top and focused on the ball. Ivan stopped it in front of her and she looked up at him.

"You try it," he whispered.

She squinted at him and swallowed hard, shaking her head.

"You can do it. Like this." Ivan held up his hand with his palm flat and his fingers pointed toward the ceiling.

Skeat held her hand in the same manner.

"Now get close behind it and it will move forward," he said, making a pushing motion with his hand.

Skeat leaned down toward the ball, inching closer while still keeping Ivan in her frame of view.

Ivan was pleased to see she understood him. "Closer," he said.

When her palm was just behind the ball, it moved forward a few inches. The child gasped and glanced at Ivan. She continued to move the ball in a circle and when she pulled her hand back, the ball followed. Ivan smiled. Skeat jerked her hand away, causing the ball to fly across the hall into the side of the enclosure. She sucked her lip, startled by the motion, and pressed herself against the wall. Ivan burst out laughing and drew the ball back to him. Ivan picked the ball up, pressing it between his palms. When he slid them apart, the ball had disappeared. Skeat's eyes narrowed.

Ivan smiled at her, but her face twisted into a scowl. She pressed her back against the energy barrier, driving her head backward against it. She pulled her legs up to her chest, wrapped her arms around them and buried her face in her knees.

"Skeat?" Ivan attempted to get her attention. He waited a few seconds before calling out to her again in a louder voice.

Nothing. She didn't even flinch, which made him wonder if she could hear him at all.

Skeat, he spoke into her mind.

She looked up curiously.

Do you understand me? Ivan asked.

Skeat nodded her head, with a look Ivan could only describe as skeptical.

Ivan covered his mouth and blocked his thoughts from her. "Can you hear me now?"

There was a subtle reaction from the child as her lip twitched while staring blankly at him. Why would she be pretending not to hear him? He decided it was time to press in. What he saw wasn't what anyone would have expected to find in a turned child.

Downstairs, Alex ushered Kitty across the living room toward the sofa. She jerked forward, slapping his hand away, and turned abruptly, stopping him in his tracks.

"You better start explaining or I'm going straight to the Alliance and turning you in!" Kitty growled at him.

Alex didn't think Kitty was in any position to make demands as aggressively as she was. His face unconsciously turned stern. "You need to be careful what you're threatening, Kitty." He sneered, leaning in toward her. She would be the one facing the Alliance's wrath if she went that route, and he didn't want that for her.

The switch in his demeanor seemed to unnerve her. She swallowed hard, taking a step back. He sensed a mixture of indignation and fear as a thin, pungent scent wafted toward him.

He watched her body language. Even though she was retreating, her stance was still combative. If she went after him, he knew her wolf wouldn't be a match for him on her best day, and he had an idea she knew it too.

"Or what?" she sneered back at him, covering her fear with more aggression. "You'll kill me?"

"No! I don't want to hurt you! After all the violence your people have endured, is my killing you out of irritation the first thing you really think about?"

"No," she replied defensively. "It's the first thing I think *you* think about."

"That's ridiculous! I was just irritated because you were threatening to go to the Alliance, and I don't think you appreciate the gravity of what's going on here." Alex knew Kitty had no idea the Alliance's highest representatives already knew about the turned from species other than human. The other delegations were the ones keeping the Rasans secret from their populations, not Alex's.

"That's because I don't know what's going on here," she replied, shaking her head vigorously. "I always knew she shouldn't be able to do the things she does, but Ivan? That's a whole other level of frightening. Your people have been lying to all of us. No species should be able to do what he's doing. And if all of you are like that…"

Alex raised his hands to quiet her. "We aren't. You saw with your own eyes that I can't do those things," he reiterated, pointing to himself.

"But some of you can, and you've been hiding it from the rest of us. The implications are huge, knowing that even some of your species are that powerful and you've hidden it from the rest of us. It makes me wonder what else you're hiding?"

Alex put his left hand on his hip and rubbed his forehead with his right. Figuring out her level of understanding or willingness to accept was a struggle for him. He stopped caring about how much trouble he was going to get into. He needed to find a plausible middle ground. On Rasa, there was never a need to lie to anyone. Here, he was strictly forbidden by the Alliance from sharing anything about the rest of the universe. Their planet, their rules. He didn't think it was fair to withhold that kind of information when human Terrans could already leave their home world on their own, albeit centuries later than he had expected. But he didn't feel like he had another option anymore. Kitty had seen things that demanded an explanation. If he didn't think she would keep his confidence, he could always make her forget the events of the morning.

"I'm gonna need a drink for this conversation," he said with resignation.

"It's seven in the morning," Kitty said, shaking her head.

Alex frowned at her, disheartened by her disapproval.

"Pour me one too," she said, in an act of surrender, walking toward the sofa. She sat cross-legged with her back against the arm, pulling a pillow across her lap. She still looked angry, but at least she hadn't run.

Alex poured two glasses and grabbed the bottle, taking it with him. He handed Kitty a glass and set the bottle on the table in front of him.

"So, what do you know about us?" Alex asked, taking a seat against the other side of the couch and slinging his arm over the back.

Kitty rolled her eyes at him. "Why are you asking me questions? You're supposed to be explaining, not asking."

"I'm just trying to figure out where I need to start. We're kind of complicated."

"We're all kinda complicated." Kitty sneered back. "You can start with what the hell is going on upstairs," she said, pointing up.

Alex took a big gulp of his drink and let out a deep sigh. "My family isn't like the species you know as vampire because we were never human. We don't even use that disgusting slur to describe ourselves. Is that complicated enough for you?"

Kitty's eyes had grown as big as saucers and her jaw hung slack. Alex waited for seconds, which felt like hours for her to respond. She suddenly sprang to her feet.

"I knew it!" she exclaimed, leaping toward Alex. "I *knew* it!" she repeated before she began regurgitating questions so quickly her words ran together. "Where are you from? How did you get here? How old are you? Are there others? What abilities …"

"Stop!" Alex cut her off, sliding himself up the armrest to escape her advance. "Jeez Kitty! Don't make me regret not wiping you!"

"Wiping me? You mean killing me?" She took a step back.

"Again, with the killing? Your memories, you twit!" Alex pushed himself to his feet.

"You can wipe my memories?!" she exclaimed, jumping toward him with excitement.

"Well, I mean, I can change bits. At least enough to make you forget everything that's happened this morning."

"What about him?" she asked, pointing up again. "Ivan?"

Alex scoffed. "Ivan could make you believe you had spent your entire life as a bird."

"Damn! That's crazy!" Kitty overemphasized the "crazy." She grabbed her glass off the table, took down the entire thing, and turned on him. "If you're not from here, how is this your house? Or should I say, how is it *his* house?" Her eyes narrowed, and she tilted her head to one side.

"He is from here. At least he always thought he was from here. I think he has three houses here if they still exist." Alex did not want to recount thousands of years of history, most of which didn't involve him.

"So, then, the vampires, sorry, the turned, know about you, and most of them left with you to go to another planet? How long have they kept that secret from the rest of us?" Kitty continued, taking on the tone of an inquisitor.

Alex was uncomfortable. He didn't mind telling her what he was. It was more difficult telling her that the human turned were hiding other Rasans' existence from the remaining Terran species. It wasn't his story to tell, but he felt he was too far in to stop now.

"When we left in the twenty-first century, tension between human governments was pretty extreme. It was also before the other abilitied species leaderships started working together, so there was no reason to reveal our existence to any of you. Sometime after that, you had your third world war, and it took centuries before humans figured out they couldn't live divided anymore. The radiation alone kept most human survivors underground for years. Coming back from the disastrous situation all of you had gotten yourselves into seemed to keep you pretty busy. Humans had only banded together because they were faced with the abilitied species Alliance that had evolved when they were in hiding, as a common enemy. At that point, revealing our existence in the universe wasn't important. Since some of our predecessors had stayed here, it was up to the inhabitants of this planet to deal with the consequences of it all." Alex shrugged.

Kitty looked at him even more intently. "From what you're saying, your own words, you could have helped us and chose not to."

"Do you seriously think that was your technology that allowed you to clean the radioactive fallout so quickly? We didn't actively help, but we didn't abandon *our* people without resources. They chose to fix this world and stay. They could have joined us and abandoned the rest of you to your own fate."

"Humans are the ones who restored this planet," Kitty said defensively.

"Humans were too busy trying to kill each other for what little scraps of livable land they thought remained to fix anything," Alex snarled back at her.

"They've learned to work together, to help each other, to build a better civilization. *We* have learned to build a better world together."

"You are not human, and they have learned nothing. They saw the damage they had caused when they built their underground cities and started harvesting fossil fuel again. A hollow crust can't stand against gravity for long, can it? As soon as they figured out how to leave here, in the face of yet another disaster they created by not living in harmony with their planet, most of them did. They gained the ability to travel through space, technology to enhance themselves and live longer, and they left all of you behind thinking you would be destroyed when the planet collapsed. Humans are as divided as they have ever been and are fighting over resources from a place they deem unfit to live on. How long do you think it's going to take before they try to come back and reclaim this little paradise from you now that we've fixed it again? Maybe a decade before they get sick of living in their domes or a century before they reproduce themselves into another crisis? They're probably already overpopulating the little habitable domes they created on otherwise desolate planets. They irresponsibly breed themselves into their own disasters. Eventually, they'll get tired of their little prisons, and they *will* come back."

"You have a very pessimistic view of what humans are capable of," Kitty sneered.

"I have a very realistic view of what humans are capable of," Alex said.

"I don't believe some altruistic interplanetary species benevolently gave us the technology to fix the planet," Kitty said, shaking her head.

"Why would I make something like that up?"

"Because you know it's something I want to believe. Because you're trying to cover something up. Maybe because you've been illegally breeding. Maybe Skeat's mother was a Galdra or a Furie, or maybe you *vampires* are genetically engineering yourselves into an unconquerable force to overtake the rest of us," Kitty replied accusingly, emphasizing the slur.

Alex dropped back onto the sofa with his head in his hands. This wasn't going the way he wanted it to at all. He needed to start over, but he knew she wouldn't listen. With a sigh, he poured himself another drink. He looked up at Kitty, then refilled her glass, setting it down on the table in front of the place where she had previously been seated. She came around reluctantly and sat, downing the entire drink, sitting the empty glass on the table, and looking at Alex. He twisted around, placing his hand on her shoulder, looking into her eyes. He dug in. Alex navigated his way to the place where her short-term memories were held and dissolved the last bits of conversation. His fingers tingled as a small whimper escaped Kitty's lips, although her blank expression hadn't changed.

Alex leaned forward, whispering his entrancement into her ear. "You will not question the lost time or remember any of the previous conversation after you said, 'Pour me one too'."

"So, what do you know about us?" Alex asked, leaning back and slinging his arm over the sofa cushion.

Kitty rolled her eyes at him. "Why are you asking me questions? You're supposed to be explaining, not asking."

"I'm just trying to figure out where I need to start. We're kind of complicated."

"We're all kinda complicated." Kitty sneered back. "You can start with what the hell is going on upstairs," she said, pointing up.

CHAPTER ELEVEN

"Ivan was turned thousands of years ago. It eventually came to light that he had powerful abilities that had been dormant before the turn. He got control of himself and lived a peaceful life for a long time, even serving as Regent after the exterminations. It was him and a few others that created the Board and most of the laws that are still in place for them today. He wanted to protect the community, so when he had the opportunity to leave the planet, he did." Alex paused a moment before adding, "on the newly colonized planet and moons, the cities are enclosed in habitation zones. Building a small habitation zone on the far side of the planet, away from the others, is the easiest way to remain isolated from the general population." Alex made sure not to make any untruthful statements, although he specifically left out that it was Rasa Ivan had gone to.

"And your mother went with him?" Kitty asked.

"A lot of us went with him."

"I remember my grandfather telling us stories about the first Regent. A lot of vampires disappeared before WW3. That was hundreds of years before planetary habitation was an option. There were rumors about aliens abducting them. We all just laughed about it," Kitty recalled.

"We had a hidden underground facility in Montana that many of my people inhabited for years." Also, a true statement, although the time they spent there was closer to five years than a few hundred.

"Why did you stay down there for so long?" she asked.

"What is time when you're immortal?" he answered, hoping this non-answer would satisfy her line of questioning.

She sighed and scratched at the front and sides of her head like she was digging at something. Before she could think of any more questions, Alex addressed the main issue.

"As far as Skeat is concerned, I don't really know how she came about."

Kitty rolled her eyes at his idiotic statement. "Seriously? You…"

"No! I know how it happens. I just don't know why she is, how she is, or, even, I guess, what she is. The only thing that makes any sense to me is that her mother may have had some dormant abilities, like Ivan had, that even she wasn't aware of." As Alex said that out loud, it seemed to be a possibility he hadn't thought of with all the surrounding commotion.

"Either way, it is still illegal for you to breed with a human. Why would you take that risk?" Kitty's question had a tone of disgust.

"Of course, I know it's illegal. Just to reiterate, I already told you I didn't do it on purpose. I don't even like children. I have an inhibitor, so I honestly didn't think she was mine when I went to claim her," Alex said. "If Gen had abilities and wasn't aware of them, it had to be wish-work. She was one-hundred percent ready for kids. It's what our last conversation was about before she broke things off with me."

The statement seemed to amuse Kitty. "She broke up with you and kept your family home? I did not see that coming."

"She didn't take my family home! Ivan knew they lived here. Her family has taken care of this property for centuries. It's not like I gave her the house," he replied defensively.

"Ooh. Sounds like I hit a nerve. Is that why you came back here? To see if she was still pining away for you?" Kitty teased.

"I came back here to go fishing."

Alex felt anger rise in Kitty even though she was smiling.

"Right. *Fishing.* Fishing for Gen," Kitty said, mocking him. Her tone sounded more terse than joking.

Alex scoffed at her. "Anyway, Ivan is going to take Skeat back with him and teach her how to control herself. I can't take her back in a shuttle because I'm afraid she'll get scared and blow it up before we can get there."

"Well, what about your port thingy?"

"It's too far. Ivan has a different way to get her back and he can keep her from blowing anything up. That's why I asked him to come," Alex admitted.

"Sounds like you have it covered now. What do you still need me for?" Kitty asked, tossing back her whole drink.

"Nothing," Ivan interrupted, coming down the stairs.

"Where's Skeat?" Kitty asked.

"Cleaning her room," Ivan replied. He turned to Kitty and added, "You're free to leave whenever you want."

"Good enough for me," Kitty answered, sounding relieved as she turned to Alex. "Where's my money?"

"Wait! Hold on," Alex exclaimed, jumping up. He wasn't ready for her to leave yet. He was more grounded around her and wasn't sure how he would be able to handle Skeat without her there.

"Excuse me?" Kitty asked. "Hold on, *why?*" She increased the distance between them. Alex sensed her urge to flee.

"You were ready to sacrifice yourself to protect her less than an hour ago and now you're ready to cash out and abandon her? What if she comes looking for you?" Alex asked.

"That's when I thought you were trying to hurt her. She's home, safe and, I suspect, pretty well protected. I am sure you are perfectly capable of catching her if she runs, though I doubt she will. He's got her cleaning her room, for Christ's sake! My job is done. I'd appreciate my payment now." Kitty answered flatly.

Alex was taken aback. "How can you so casually be done? Don't you care what happens to her?"

Kitty laughed so hard she snorted. "How did that sentence not burn when it fell out of your mouth? You can't even commit to a color, much less a person, and you're calling me out?" she asked, pointing at his black attire. "I go where I'm needed. There are a lot of other kids out there who need me right now. She is not one of them."

Alex opened his mouth to speak. When no words found him, he shut it again.

Ivan stepped in. "We appreciate everything you've done for the child," he said to Kitty when he made it to the bottom of the stairs. "Alex, pay her what you agreed upon."

"She stayed less than half the time she agreed to, so I'm only paying her half."

Kitty began to protest and was cut off by Ivan.

"Pay her what you agreed upon," Ivan repeated in a commanding tone.

Alex begrudgingly pulled out his device and entered the transaction as Ivan approached Kitty, holding out his hand.

"Good luck with your next hunt," Ivan said as Kitty reached out to shake his hand.

Before their fingers had touched, Ivan began to press into her mind. In the time it had taken to complete the handshake, he had rewritten her memories and removed the portions from upstairs she shouldn't have seen. He changed the event and replaced it with mundane routines she would not find remarkable in any way. Before he let go, while still holding her gaze, the corners of his mouth turned imperceivably downward. "Ida, permanently erase the conversation from Ms. Winterclaw's device from this morning."

"The designated recording and backup have been permanently erased," Ida replied.

Ivan took a step back, smiled and wished Kitty well on her journey. Alex was slightly confused and angry as he finished the credit transfer. He didn't give away more than slight irritation to Kitty.

"Would you like us to take you somewhere?" Ivan offered.

"I prefer walking. Thanks," Kitty replied and headed for the door.

The moment Kitty was outside and out of hearing range, Alex turned on Ivan. "What in all hells was that?"

"Guess you've been working on that 'not seeing everything as a threat' thing. She recorded all of your conversations." Ivan snickered, heading back up to check on Skeat's progress.

"Shit!" Alex exclaimed. "That is exactly why I don't trust outsiders."

"Trust goes both ways, Alex. She already knew about our ability to entrance, and she wanted to make sure you weren't doing it to her." Ivan's words trailed off as he made his way down the upstairs hallway.

"You entranced her too!" Alex yelled up at him.

Ivan immediately appeared back at the top of the stairs. "I entranced her to protect our pact with the Alliance. You entranced her because you told her things you shouldn't have, and you didn't like the way your conversation was going. I wouldn't have needed to do anything if you had told her it wasn't her business and sent her on her way."

"She was helping me. I had to tell her something."

"No. You didn't have to, you wanted to. And what you want isn't important right now." Ivan finished his statement by disappearing back down the hall.

Alex went to the kitchen to grab a coffee. He was disappointed in himself. It was a hard line to walk between trusting people and being paranoid about everyone. Ivan was right. If he had only handled the first conversation better, he wouldn't have had to entrance her. He hadn't wanted to, but it had gotten so out of hand he had seen no other option. Alex despised being away from Rasa and needing to make these kinds of decisions. Skirting the truth was never something he was good at. Being stoic was something he was usually very good at. For some reason, with Kitty, he wanted to spill his guts. He couldn't understand his urge to tell her everything.

He made his way out to the back deck for some air. Something about being amongst the glistening mountain tops funneling clear, cool pine scented air toward him made it easier to clear his head. After standing for a few more minutes, he took his cup and headed up the stairs.

Barely halfway up, a knock on the front door interrupted Alex. He sensed a wolf, excitedly wondering what had made Kitty return.

"Did you forget something?" Alex asked, pulling the door open. To his surprise, it was not Kitty.

"Expecting someone else I take it?" the large man at the front door asked.

"Cyras?" Alex took a step back, surprised to see the Ultimate Alpha at his front door. "What are you doing here?"

Cyras sighed. "Business."

"Official?" Alex asked nervously. It's not every day the head of the Shifter Delegation to the Alliance shows up at your door unannounced.

Cyras let out a bellowing laugh that shook the door frame. "I'm retired from all that mess, Alex. The only duties left for me are of the Elder Gamma variety. I'd like to spend my last few centuries lounging in luxury."

Cyras' demeanor did not bring Alex any comfort. "What kind of Gamma business has brought you to my door, Cyras?" Alex remained in the doorway without granting the man entry.

"Why are you so nervous? What are you hiding in there?" Cyras leaned forward, sniffing at the air.

"You didn't answer my question, Cyras." Alex leaned against the door frame, sipping his coffee. He was nervous. Not about facing off with the old wolf. It would be a decent enough challenge, but Alex knew he could take Cyras. Alex needed to be sure he hadn't come for Skeat.

"I was on my way to see Ivan, but I do have a bone to pick with you. You entranced my granddaughter, Kaitriona," Cyras said, leaning closer to Alex as Kitty stepped out from behind one of the porch columns.

Alex laughed and shook his head. "What would make you think that?"

Kitty stepped in between Cyras and Alex, flashing the latter a wicked little grin. "You didn't entrance my wolf, idiot." She smirked wider as she pushed past him into the house.

CHAPTER TWELVE

"I didn't have a choice, Kitty," Alex said as he paced in front of the pair that had seated themselves on his sofa.

"Everybody has a choice."

Alex stopped and faced Kitty. "Look, they're not my rules. I told you something I shouldn't have." He glanced at Cyras. "I told you something the Alliance forbids you from knowing about us. I had to maintain the treaty and entrance you to eliminate the information." Alex crossed his arms in defense of his actions.

"But you didn't!" Kitty exclaimed, jumping to her feet. "You only entranced the human part of my consciousness. You didn't entrance my wolf. Did you want me to remember, or are you just stupid?"

He stepped closer to Kitty. "I didn't know the wolf had her own memories, so I guess I'm just stupid!" The accusation and the amused look on Cyras's face irritated Alex.

"Excuse me, would you mind keeping your voices down? Skeat doesn't like the angry vibe going on between the two of you," Ivan interjected from the top of the staircase, drawing everyone's attention. Skeat was peeking around from behind Ivan.

Alex spun back to Kitty, ignoring Ivan's request. "Are you going to call Ivan stupid, too?"

Kitty scoffed. "For what?"

"He also entranced you," Alex said with a smug grin.

Kitty's eyes jetted from side to side for a few seconds. "Maybe he did, but it looks like he was bright enough to get both sides, unlike you." She sneered, poking a finger into Alex's chest.

Cyras chuckled again. "All right, you two. That's enough. Just tell her the rest of it."

Alex looked back at Ivan. Kitty shifted her weight onto one foot and put her hand on her hip, looking expectantly at Alex.

Ivan shrugged as he walked down the stairs. "It's not my call. We're not the ones hiding anything here. If he says to tell her, then tell her."

Cyras added with a mischievous look, "but do it outside. The grown-ups have something to discuss."

"I'm older than all of you put together," Alex retorted, glaring at Cyras.

"I guess age and maturity don't go hand in hand with your species, then," Cyras said gruffly.

Ivan intervened. "I'll just take Cyras to my office. Why don't you make Skeat some breakfast while you're letting Kitty in on our background?"

Kitty picked Skeat up and took her to the kitchen, leaving Alex to stare at Ivan.

"Well?" Ivan asked.

"I'd like to know what he's doing here," Alex answered, nodding to Cyras.

"Kitty called him yesterday. I saw it when I scanned her memories and I need him to find someone for me. As soon as she told him I was here, I knew he'd come." Ivan shrugged.

"So, you knew who she was?"

"I knew the second she bit me. I just didn't see any reason to bring it up at that point. Last time I saw her, she was just a pup. She didn't seem to know I was the same Ivan who used to be Regent, so I didn't feel the need to say anything." Ivan shrugged again and turned to lead Cyras to the office.

Alex stood in the middle of the room dumbfounded, watching Ivan traverse the hall toward the office. It wasn't really the question he had meant to ask.

Ivan turned back before he entered the room. "Oh, and in case you were wondering, she was looking for a chip of stone she had lost. Something about pictures," he said, before disappearing into the room and shutting the door.

Alex reached into his front pocket. His fingers grazed the cold, hard mineral disk, knowing exactly what Skeat had wanted.

When Alex strolled into the room, Kitty was standing at the stove beating her frustrations out on a bowl of eggs. It infuriated her more to see him looking so smug, walking past her toward Skeat. He leaned down to where she was playing on the floor with a puzzle she had extracted from a cabinet at the end of the buffet.

How did he have the balls to ignore her while she was fuming at him the way she was? He pulled something out of his pocket, gaining wide-eyed attention from Skeat. The girl grabbed at whatever it was he held in his hand, only to have him pull it away. With that fucking irritatingly charming grin Kitty couldn't stand, he had elicited a pout from Skeat.

Alex's face turned more serious, making sure he had Skeat's attention. "We don't break things when we're angry," he said. "Do you understand?"

Skeat nodded back, biting on her lower lip. Alex placed the object in one palm and waved the other hand over the top, projecting a three-dimensional image of space and stars. Skeat's expression went wild with delight, and she reached out, looking up at Alex, pleading with her huge green eyes. He moved his hand closer toward her, allowing her to take it. He pointed toward the back doors.

"Go play on the deck until breakfast is ready," he said.

Skeat hopped up and ran outside, balancing the image in front of her with a wide smile plastered on her face. Alex turned and walked toward Kitty. As he approached the island counter, the smile reemerged while Kitty pretended to ignore him.

"I know you're mad at me. I didn't do it to hurt you."

Kitty scoffed and shifted her weight to the other foot, beating the eggs even harder, if that was possible. She was whipping them so hard and fast that her hand was getting sore.

"I'm sorry. I told you more than I was supposed to, and I didn't know what else to do," Alex offered sincerely.

Kitty slammed the bowl down on the counter, picked up a knife and turned sharply around, making Alex gasp. He froze in place with his hands a few inches above the counter. She made sure the joy she felt from his reaction didn't reach her face.

"Someone finally learned what a genuine apology should sound like," she replied curtly, turning her back on him again. She began chopping vegetables with a vicious fervor. "This is the part where you begin speaking," she added with a satisfied grin she knew he couldn't see.

Alex drew out the air that had unexpectedly invaded his lungs only moments ago.

"You said you were never human, so what the hell were you?" She turned, pointing the knife at him again. "And don't fucking lie to me or play your little twisted mind games," she added, turning her focus back to her chopping. She was angry, disappointed, curious and a whole mixture of other things she didn't want to be in that moment. Why did his distrust make her feel so out of control? She didn't give two shits about his opinion yesterday. She would have expected him to lie to her then, but not today. Today, she felt they had built some trust.

"Your grandfather had five hundred years to tell you and didn't. I've only known you for a day. Why are you so mad at me?" Alex's voice sounded irritated.

"Don't you try to turn this on him! He may have never told me, but he also didn't lie to me or try to make me forget an entire conversation!" Kitty growled back, looking over her shoulder, waving the knife.

"I didn't lie to you either. Technically," Alex defended.

"I don't really know that yet, do I? You did try to make me forget, though." Kitty stopped chopping and leaned forward on her hands. She felt betrayed. She didn't even know this smug, entitled asshole sitting behind her and yet she still felt a deep wash of betrayal. The lying she may have been able to deal with. What she couldn't forgive was the audacity he took with violating her thoughts.

"I know I did, and I know it was wrong of me to entrance you. The Alliance forbade us from telling the other species what we really were. If others find out, they may try to force the old ones to leave the only home they know. Some of them are afraid of us," Alex explained.

"Who? The old ones? Who are they, anyway?"

"No, the old ones aren't afraid of us. They're the original turned from this planet. The other abilitied species are afraid of us," Alex answered.

Kitty picked up her knife and resumed chopping. "What exactly are you?" She didn't know if she wanted the answer, even though she felt she needed it.

"Me personally, or all of us?"

Kitty sighed, slowing her chopping. "Let's start with you personally." She grimaced when she felt her stomach doing back flips inside of her. Kitty could feel an urgency to know all about this man whom she had begun to loathe. The need to understand and the need to run created a conflict she was very uncomfortable with. She again shifted her weight to the other foot.

"Well, I'm Æsir, from Asgard," he said.

Alex was stunned by Kitty's quick motion as she twisted toward him, the knife stopping close to his face. He expected to see anger instead of the intently perplexed expression that appeared.

"What?" she finally spat out after close to ten seconds of her silently shaking her head. "Like the comic books? Next, you're going to tell me Thor is your father. Do you think I'm stupid? Even I know that's mythology."

She turned her conversation inward. *Oh ... my ... God! He's pathological! And he thinks I'm stupid!*

Give him a chance to explain! She argued on the other side of the conversation.

Don't you dare defend him! You have always had horrible judgment when it comes to men!

But you have to listen to him! He's our …

Don't you fucking dare even think that! He is not now, and he never will be! Kitty scolded herself, feeling the wolf side of her personality recoil back into the recesses of her mind, whimpering.

"That would be ridiculous. He's my father's half-brother. My mother would never," Alex replied with a stoic expression. He was trying as hard as he could not to laugh. He didn't want to laugh at her, but the way she was looking at him was so damned amusing. There was no way she could know any of those stories she heard as a child had a basis in reality. He might be an asshole, but he wasn't intentionally cruel.

The look that slid over her face told him she didn't believe a word of it.

"I can prove it," he said, holding his hands up in a surrender position.

"How could you possibly do that?"

"I can share a memory with you?" he said, phrasing it more as a question than a statement.

"If you make a single move to touch me, I will stab you in the face." Kitty glared at him, slipping the knife forward until the tip touched his cheek.

"I'm not going to touch you," Alex said calmly, not daring to move.

"Well?" Kitty asked, matching his tone.

"Uh, I need to take my device out of my pocket," he said and slowly moved one hand toward the side pocket of his pants while keeping the other in the air.

Kitty pulled the knife away and stepped back to lean against the counter behind her. Alex placed his TAC down in front of him, clicking the two ends together, causing a holographic screen to protrude from the metal base. He pulled at the corners, allowing the screen to expand, hovering in the space between them. He concentrated on linking his thoughts to the device. A blur of images crossed the screen until finally landing on a garden scene filled with vivid foliage.

The scene was surreal. Alex hadn't thought about this place in centuries. Deep green grass surrounded by unusual shades of foliage speckled with flowers of shapes and colors foreign to anything he has seen since. The frame moved upward, revealing a cobalt blue sky filled with a huge orange sun. It was breathtaking until the serenity was broken by the blade of a sword slashing in front, causing Kitty to jump in surprise. A second blade came up from the bottom of the frame, blocking the first, as Alex swung his sword upward. A third sword blade moved through sideways, lopping off a large section of shrubbery as Alex jerked backward without losing his balance.

"Það er nóg! Eyðilagðir þú virkilega blóm mín?" A familiar woman's voice had broken through the sound of clanging metal, making Alex's breathing hitch in his throat for a moment.

"What did she say?"

Kitty's voice had snapped him away from the images in front of him. Alex half smiled, although his eyes looked sad. Kitty thought she saw a blush of embarrassment.

"That's the way I remember it. I ... uh, need to make an adjustment so you can understand it."

Kitty nodded, watching the thought set itself back a few seconds.

> "That's enough! Did you really just ruin my flowers?" came his mother's chiding, and somehow also amused voice.
>
> "It was Mikkel. He still doesn't have control of those broad swings!" Alex teased Mikkel, who looked exactly like Alex, only a few years younger than the man standing in front of her now.
>
> "Aleksander, don't make fun of your brother," she admonished softly as Alex looked up at her. He always remembered her being rather plain, but pretty with long dark hair braided down her back. She appeared to be in her mid to late thirties, but at that point in time she was already quite ancient in mortal terms. What really stood out were those huge, clear green eyes. No one could ever deny that she was, at the very least, related to Alex and his brothers.
>
> "Yeah, if you weren't hiding in the bushes like a scared little child, I wouldn't have had to swing so

wide," Mikkel teased back, slapping Alex in the chest with the flat side of his sword. As the sword was pulled back, Alex observed Kitty focusing on the details. It was huge and had intricate designs surrounding rune inscriptions on the blade. The pommel was thick and sturdy, supporting a bright silver shaft wrapped with braided black metal.

Erik emerged from the bushes on the right side, looking exactly like the other two, shaking his head. The only visual difference between the two that were in front of him was a few of their tattoos were different, although most of the ones from this angle were the same.

"Yes, mother," Alex replied.

"Come then. Odin is waiting for you. The feast is about to begin," she said, signaling them to follow her.

"Did she just say Odin? Like the mythological god, Odin?" Kitty asked as Alex paused the memory again.

"Not so mythological when he's your grandfather," Alex quipped.

"Right," Kitty said skeptically.

"He's not like the stories. I mean, he ruled our people and controlled several planets within the kingdom, but your books get so much more wrong than they do right."

"Uh-huh," she replied, adhering to the same tone as before.

"Just watch." Alex pointed, continuing the memory.

The triplets walked through winding garden paths following their mother, with Alex in the rear. They were dressing as they walked, as though it were a normal occurrence, tossing their swords and other gear to each other to free their hands in a succinct, unspoken rhythm. When they turned the last corner, the huge palace came into view at the top of a gently sloping hill.

Kitty gasped at the sight of it towering high into the skies. It was larger than any castle she had ever seen. It wasn't at all what she expected to see from supposed Viking gods, but neither was the flowing white pantsuit their mother wore.

The sun glistened off the polished white stone with gold and glass towers. Alex's memory was so detailed that he could physically imagine the sun's warmth embracing his face as they journeyed across the field and arrived at the main lawn. The short walk across the grass ended at the lower servant's entrance, filled with crates of food and casks of wine and mead lining the walls. There was still plenty of space for the men to walk side by side, leaving room for others to pass. The cobbled stone floor of the hallway echoed under their boots. Their walk continued past dozens of people he remembered fondly, carrying trays, glasses, crates of food and other wares one would expect to see at a feast.

"A quarter hour," their mother called out, continuing her path forward as the men turned left, heading down a much narrower corridor and up several flights of stairs. He had almost forgotten how no-nonsense she had been back then. No need for useless conversation if it could be imparted with a look. The fourth-floor landing opened up to a circular hall with deep-set windows on one side and three doors on the other. Each of the men took a separate entrance in silence.

Once inside his room, the first thing Alex did was to take a cloth and wipe down the blade of his sword, placing it firmly into a bracket mounted on the white stone wall. It didn't matter if you used your blade or not; if you unsheathed it, you cleaned it. If you did use it, you sharpened it. But he didn't have time for that now. He would do it when he returned from the feast.

It had been so long since he had dove into this memory. It brought a smile to his face.

Now it was time for him to prepare for what would turn out to be a long night. He pulled off his shirt and slipped his thumbs into the sides of his pants…

"I don't think I need to see this part!" Kitty exclaimed, covering her eyes.

"We haven't even gotten to the feast yet. I promise you won't doubt me after that," Alex said.

"All you've proved so far is that you are an identical triplet, rich beyond imagination, and grew up in a place surrounded by flowers I have never seen. Then again, if you are older than Ivan and my grandpa combined …"

"And you," Alex cut in.

"And me. Those could very well be a species of flora that has become extinct," Kitty said, raising an eyebrow at him. She was pragmatic and skeptical.

"How would you explain the palace construction then? Or the metalwork on the swords? I saw you staring at those. They didn't work fine metals like that in those times. Not on this planet anyway," Alex pointed out.

"How do you explain the pyramids? They were considered very advanced construction that was thought to be too technical for their time," Kitty countered.

"I can if you would rather me do that than show you the rest of this." Alex gestured toward the screen.

Kitty glared at him.

"Shall we continue?" Alex asked.

"Skip the part where you take your clothes off and look in the mirror." Kitty glared impertinently.

"As you wish." Alex turned back to his task, skipping forward a bit.

> Alex was seated at a long stone table elevated at the front of the main hall. He never enjoyed being up here for these events. Everyone ogled The Three as if they were a sideshow. His brothers sat to his right, his mother to his left followed by their father, their blind uncle

Hödr and grandmother Frigg.

Alex was watching his grandfather, Odin, at the center of the table. The older man was adorned in a dark blue, well fitted long sleeve shirt and a golden chain with a large sapphire. His hair was shoulder-length and silvery white, with a matching well-trimmed beard. Once he stood, the music stopped, and the room fell silent. Alex turned his attention out over the hall at six long tables perpendicular to their own, holding another twenty guests each. The food- and drink-laden tables were covered with fine, colorful linens. Plates of silver and gold were laid at each setting and the drinks were served in fine glass. The hall was easily as long as the ceiling was high. Overall, it was an ostentatious hall with space to dance and an orchestra at the far end.

He looked past his grandfather to see more of Odin's sons from women other than Frigg.

Thor sat at his left hand followed by his wife Sif, then Víðarr and his wife Solveig, Tyr and last was Hermod. There was also an empty seat for Váli who had been notably unwelcome at these or any other events ever since he tried to kill Frigg, yet the empty seat remained. It was likely one of Odin's mind games showing everyone that if he didn't hesitate to cut his own son out of his life, no one was safe from his ire.

"Why am I hearing your thoughts? You're sitting there in a room full of people doing nothing, and I can hear you narrating who they are." Kitty's voice again stirred him from his presentation. "You promised not to manipulate my thoughts!" She had been staring at him for the last several minutes without him noticing.

"I'm not manipulating your thoughts; I'm just talking to you. It's what I was thinking about at the moment. No one was speaking yet. Do you want to stare at a screen and not know who's in the room or what's going on?" How in all hells did she think he was going to be able to translate everything for her if he didn't speak telepathically to her?

"Are those people even who you say they are? They look so normal, not like gods at all."

"You didn't seriously expect them to look like comic book characters, did you? We don't wear tights, dead animals, or giant horned helmets," he said, curling his lip back.

Kitty broke eye contact with him, her cheeks flushed with embarrassment. "No, I guess I just … I don't know. I thought they'd be less sophisticated, okay?"

Alex didn't hold his laughter back this time. "We have been able to travel through this universe since before this planet even had humans on it and you thought we'd somehow look more primitive?"

"You don't have to be a jerk about it." Kitty looked back up, sulking.

"I didn't mean to laugh." Alex sighed. "Look, let's take a break and let you wrap your head around this. We can finish after breakfast, okay?"

"Fine. We have plenty of time and I don't think you want Skeat to starve just so we can argue. But don't think you're off the hook. I have a lot more questions and we haven't even gotten to the turned yet," Kitty spoke as she turned on the griddle and pulled out the utensils. She groaned to herself. Why was she so invested in this? If she was smart, she would walk out the door right now and not look back. What did she care whether any of it was true or not? It's not like she was ever going to see it anyway, was it?

"Make a list of your questions. I'll make coffee," Alex said. He didn't know why it felt so important to him that she knew he wasn't lying to her. All she had done since he met her was question and challenge him. The only reason he had to speak to her at all was her attachment to Skeat.

CHAPTER THIRTEEN

Ivan grabbed two glasses from the cabinet and poured them without asking Cyras if he wanted one. He already knew the answer to that question. It may have been hundreds of years since they had seen each other, but that was something he was certain he still knew about his old friend. He sat one in front of Cyras and took a seat behind his large, heavy desk. After all this time, it still felt comfortable for him.

"Do you think they know yet?" Cyras asked.

"I'm sure she does, but Alex? Absolutely not. He can be slow with that type of thing," Ivan replied, joining Cyras in a hearty laugh.

"So, what about the girl? All the Alliance has been told is that she's traumatized and isn't speaking. Kitty had a little more to say about her." Cyras tipped his glass toward Ivan and took a sip.

"That's what I need your help with."

Cyras raised an eyebrow at the statement. "What could I possibly help you with?"

"I need an elemental reader. Are you still in touch with Aribella?" Ivan asked pensively.

"Ivan, you have the skill to delve into the most difficult minds and change thoughts. Why would you need a reader? Aribella isn't as spry as she once was. She'd need a compelling reason to come all the way here," Cyras pointed out.

"I saw something I don't understand. She's an open telepath, which we've dealt with before, although not in a child this old."

"And?" Cyras urged.

"She doesn't seem to be able to hear speech, but she still hears sounds and thoughts? She should be able to speak, but she doesn't appear to have the connection to form words. Her telepathy seems to be incoming only, which may be tied to her speech. I know that doesn't make any sense. I've never run across anything like it before and I don't know what I'm looking at. It's a big knot where everything looks like it's tied together in a way that it shouldn't be," Ivan admitted.

"Why don't you take her back to Rasa? You certainly have people there who can figure this out, don't you?" Cyras asked.

"I will eventually. I'm not sure this is the right time. She's lost a lot and moving her again might not be the best thing for her. Until we figure out her communication issues, moving her is a safety concern as well," Ivan replied.

"A safety concern?" Cyras inquired.

"She's an energy grafter," Ivan twisted in his chair as Cyras's eyes widened. "The safest place for her and everyone else, for the time being at least, is with me. I also think it would be detrimental to take her away from here until we can explain to her what's happening."

"I see," Cyras contemplated, rubbing his chin. "What kind of danger does the child pose?" he asked as his mind shifted into Alpha mode. It was a reflex he couldn't easily shake.

"None that I can't contain, Cyras," Ivan replied, assuredly meeting his gaze.

"Old habits, friend," Cyras conceded.

"I understand. I have a few of those myself," Ivan said with a lighthearted glint in his eyes. "Now, what about Aribella?"

"What about Sadie? Can't you use that to scan the girl?" Cyras asked.

"I already ruled that option out. We only have Sadie's security module here, and they limit our communication devices in that capacity. I'd have to take her back for a full scan or have Leo bring medical devices here. I'm not sure she'd be comfortable with either option," Ivan explained.

Cyras rubbed his chin again. He wasn't sure if bringing more people into this situation was the best idea; although, if anyone could be trusted it would be Aribella. "I'll ask her. It may take some time though," he finally said, bringing his eyes back to Ivan.

"I'll give you some privacy then." Ivan drank the last of his drink and rose from his chair to leave Cyras to the solitude of the room.

When Ivan turned the corner at the end of the hall, he saw Skeat eating breakfast, watching a photo display rotating in front of her. That must have been what she had been looking for, he thought to himself. Kitty was putting away food from the griddle and Alex was nowhere in sight.

"You hungry? There's plenty left," Kitty offered.

"Sure. Thanks," he answered, looking around the room. "Where's Alex?"

"He needed some air," Kitty replied and started filling a plate.

"Did you get all your answers?" Ivan asked, taking a seat at the counter next to Skeat, who glanced up to acknowledge him before moving back to her display.

"Not even close," Kitty huffed.

"Anything I can help with?" Ivan asked.

"He showed me part of his memory of a feast of some sort, and he tried to tell me they were gods." Kitty rolled her eyes.

"Alex would never tell you his family members were gods. I think you misunderstood."

"Well, he didn't exactly say they were gods. He said they were normal immortals that some on this planet thought of as gods. How ridiculous is that?" Kitty scoffed.

Ivan glanced down at Skeat, making the decision to move this conversation to a more private mode, and created a direct link with Kitty, blocking Skeat. *If he was showing you his family, then what he said was true.*

Why should I believe you any more than I believe him? Kitty leered at him.

Because I don't care what you think. Your grandfather said to tell you. Without the hindrance of the Alliance's secret to protect, I have no reason to lie. Ivan stared blankly back at her.

You mean your secret, don't you? Kitty retorted.

We never wanted to be a secret from the other abilitied species. The Alliance thought if others were aware of what we had become, they would want to join us and leave this planet, too. That would have been very disruptive for some of the other species. May have even ended in a war amongst them.

Disruptive how? Kitty asked.

Well, say half of your pack decided to take the turn and leave with us. How do you think the packs surrounding your territory would react? What about your own pack leaders? Do you think they'd be happy about losing half their pack members? Who do you think they would blame since they couldn't get to us?

I didn't think about it that way. Kitty said.

We had to create a pact to not reveal ourselves to anyone outside of the Alliance in order to let those of our species who wanted to stay behind do so in peace, Ivan explained without breaking eye contact.

Why does my grandfather think I need to know any of this? I'll never be a member of the Alliance. My Aunt is Alpha, those duties will fall to her children,

That is not a question I can answer. Ivan didn't feel it was his place to answer for another's motives.

Kitty paused, trying to think about what Ivan had said. Her grandfather told them to tell her. Ivan was right. Neither he nor Alex had a reason to lie to her now. She was only disappointed that her grandfather hadn't been the one to say anything. Even her aunt had to know. How many others knew and how could they have left her out? Could that be at least part of the reason why she was so angry at Alex, because he had excluded her too?

Skeat finished her breakfast and got down from the stool. As she ran past Ivan, he put his hand out to stop her. She looked up at him indignantly.

Ivan looked down to meet her eyes. He thought she could understand if he spoke while looking at her. "Where do you think you're going?"

Skeat pointed up with her free hand as she balanced the holographs on the other.

"Put your dishes in the sink first," he gently ordered with a grin that made his eyes twinkle.

Skeat nodded and did as she was told. Ivan saw she was compliant enough when she was happy, while also wondering what he needed to do to keep her in that state to avoid another episode like the one this morning. Once she had ascended to the top of the stairs, he moved his attention back to Kitty, who seemed to have formed another coherent thought.

"What had you become? You said the Alliance didn't want the others to find out what you had become." Kitty was very good at picking the important parts out of a conversation, even if her own feelings distracted her.

Ivan glanced up at her wistfully. "Free."

Kitty watched him for what seemed like a long time as he gathered his thoughts. He looked like he had become so incredibly sad and old in those few minutes as she waited.

"When Alex's mother and I became mates, it changed everything. Her blood changed everything. Her light changed us all," Ivan recounted at a slow, intentional pace.

As much as she wanted to push, Kitty didn't want to interrupt.

Ivan looked up to meet her eyes. "As vampires, our thirst was insatiable. The thirst rules everything. No matter how evolved or benevolent you believe yourself to be, when the thirst comes, it can't be resisted. For a long time, we made sure to stave off the thirst by taking smaller quantities more often. It worked well and also ensured that we wouldn't need to kill to feed. But when we were able to create a blood alternative from *her* blood, it took the thirst away completely. Her blood turned us into something else altogether."

A prideful smile skimmed Ivan's lips, slipping off as quickly as it came.

He continued, "the light, serenity and even the knowledge that came from her swept through our connection like a virus infecting us all. We evolved into an entirely different species. Our minds expanded and for most of us, this tiny little planet filled with fear and hatred simply seemed too small."

"Is that why you left? How did you do it? Leave, I mean. How did you head out into the universe with no idea where you were going?" Kitty's curiosity grew as she felt the truth in his words. This broken man in front of her, on the verge of tears, couldn't be lying. She wanted to know more about Alex's mother. The woman who hadn't appeared special at all in Alex's memory must have been very special indeed. Kitty couldn't ask the question she really wanted to. She wouldn't ask that of him.

"For every miraculous event, there is always an equally devastating one. As our species was being elevated, the Æsir were succumbing to tragedy. Their great war ended their world. Just over one-hundred survivors made their way here. They took the lead. They knew what was out there, and they knew how to get there. We joined together, forming the beginnings of a species that has thrived throughout The Everything for hundreds of years." He breathed out heavily and cocked his eye at her. "That is an extremely succinct version of how we ended up where we are today."

Ivan rubbed the side of his head, bringing himself out of whatever mournful, torturous place his mind had wandered, and smiled at Kitty.

Ivan stood, pushing his untouched plate back toward her. "I'll leave the remainder of your enlightenment to Alex. I think I've had all the memories I can bear for one day."

Kitty unconsciously rolled her eyes at the mention of Alex's name.

"What was that look for?" Ivan asked.

"I'm sorry. It wasn't you. It's Alex. He's so flippant and irresponsible." She grimaced.

"The one thing you probably can't say about Alex is that he is irresponsible. He carries the weight of all our people on his shoulders," Ivan replied.

"What's that supposed to mean?"

"It means that he thinks he is responsible for the demise of the entire Æsir population. He thinks if he could have kept his brother in check, he never would have made their grandfather angry, and they wouldn't have been sent away to cool their heels when their world was destroyed. If Odin hadn't made that one decision, The Three would have been in Asgard when it was attacked, and there is no doubt in anyone's mind, their attackers would have been the ones defeated. The opposite side of that is, if Asgard had survived, our current planet, Rasa would have never risen. The balance of the miraculous and devastating tears at him and he is the only one of his brothers that has not been able to come to terms with it. He feels personally responsible for each and every one of us." With that calm, matter-of-fact statement, Ivan turned and walked away, leaving Kitty stunned.

Back in the living room, Cyras was standing at the window with his back to Ivan. "I hadn't realized you used her blood to make CB. Makes a lot more sense now." His tone was relaxed, and he made the statement without turning around. "Could you have used blood from any of the others if you had it?"

Ivan smiled, wondering how much of the conversation he had heard. "Probably." He didn't see why blood from the other Æsir wouldn't have worked to sate the thirst, although the end result wouldn't have been the same. The turned wouldn't have been drawn in by her light. It was a rabbit hole he wasn't interested in descending. "Is Aribella coming?" he asked, guiding the conversation in a direction he preferred.

"You knew before you asked me to find her she wouldn't be able to stay away," Cyras continued, looking out the window as Ivan stepped up beside him.

"I'm assuming she's coming soon." Ivan nodded in the direction Cyras was looking.

"Her shuttle should be departing from Big Bear Island soon. She'll be here within the hour." Cyras turned to study Ivan's reaction, but there was none.

"I'm going to go up and make sure Skeat stays calm. Let me know when she gets here," he said, patting Cyras on the shoulder before he walked away.

When he got upstairs, he leaned into the door frame of Skeat's room. She was sitting at her desk with the holographic display open and her drawing pad out. Ivan smiled at the complete turn the scene of this room had taken since the morning. Not so much as one pillow was out of place. Ivan chewed at the skin on the side of his fingernail, trying to decide how to approach the conversation he needed to have with her.

"Skeat, we have a visitor coming. Is that going to cause a problem?" Ivan studied her closely, and although her head didn't move, he could see the corner of her eye fill with a painfully familiar green before changing back to white as she momentarily cut her eye in his direction. He moved closer, leaning against the edge of the desk so he could see her entire face.

When he spoke, he leaned forward into her field of view. "Skeat, are we going to have a problem with our visitor?"

Skeat raised her eyes to meet his, and she grimaced.

"She's coming to help figure out how to understand you. Promise me you won't try to hurt her."

Skeat turned her head away and huffed loudly.

Ivan placed his finger under her chin and gently moved her gaze back to meet his. "Promise you won't hurt her."

Skeat glowered and nodded curtly, jerking her head away from his hand. It seemed as good an agreement as he was going to get. He couldn't blame her for being distrustful or angry. Her mother and grandfather were both dead and strangers had taken over her home. The last three months leading up to this point had been no better, with her being shuttled from one noisy, torturous place to another. Of course, she would feel as though she had no one left and nowhere to go. She must be so lost inside her little world. Ivan felt deep sorrow for everything she had gone through.

He pushed himself to his feet and scanned the room once again. The furnishings were the same as they had been when it was Alex's room. Paint and fabrics had changed, but little else. He made his way to a window seat on the opposite side of the room. It was positioned so he could watch Skeat and the driveway at the same time.

It wasn't long before a shuttle hovered up the narrow stretch over the driveway. Before it had time to drop its landing gear, the passenger hatch opened, revealing a very aged Aribella. This was the part Ivan hated the most about dealing with mortals. Even a semi-mortal as ancient as Aribella was destined to die. Once she was fully out of the shuttle, Ivan could see how unkind the centuries had been to her. Her once dark lustrous hair had faded to a dreary gray from which fell cavernous creases throughout her face. Surprisingly, her posture remained straight and her hazel eyes clear as they met his through the window glass. Aribella nodded and reached back to retrieve her staff from the storage compartment.

Ahh, that staff. He smiled to himself when he caught the glint of sunlight on metal. It was the first thing he had seen of a very naïve, young Aribella all that time ago. For any type of conjurer, elemental, witch, or whatever the vogue term was being used these days, the staff was their best piece of equipment. It was a walking stick, grounding stick, spell holder, spit, drying rack, fishing pole, and weapon. Of the millions of uses it was capable of, the most important to its owner was spell keeping. Each was personalized with spells carved into the metal, ready to be brought forth at the owner's whim. It was a much different whim which brought that staff to meet Ivan's unsuspecting face on a moonless night at the edge of a forest. But that was a memory for another time.

Ivan moved away from the window, walking past Skeat toward the door. There was no need to disturb her just yet. He wanted to discuss something with Aribella first.

The old woman was already standing in the entryway when Ivan reached the bottom of the stairs.

"My, my. I never thought there would come a day when you had a problem you couldn't figure out on your own," Aribella said as she surveyed Ivan from head to toe.

"It's good to see you, Aribella. It's been far too long," Ivan replied, moving closer toward her and Cyras.

"That is entirely your fault. I have gone nowhere, but I've heard countless tales of your adventures," she said with an admonishing tone while she grinned at him.

Ivan dropped his head bashfully. "You're right. It is completely my fault," he apologized. "Please forgive me."

"Nothing at all to forgive. Truth be told, I'd be out there if I had the opportunity." Aribella graciously replied with a mischievous twinkle in her eye.

The trio turned in the direction of an exasperated scoff coming from the kitchen. "Am I the only one on this entire planet who was oblivious to what was going on?" Kitty asked, appearing irritated with her hand on her hip and her head tilted to the side.

"Kitty! That is rude. Aribella holds a seat on the Alliance, and she has known Ivan much longer than I have," Cyras admonished.

"Cyras," Aribella cooed, patting Cyras' arm. "Leave the poor girl alone. No one takes it well when they first hear about them." Aribella turned to Kitty. "Kitty, would you be a dear and go retrieve the child's father for us, please?"

"Yes, Madame Goodwind," Kitty replied as her cheeks flushed red. She nodded and turned to the doors on the other side of the kitchen.

Once Kitty had stepped out onto the deck, Aribella turned back to Cyras and Ivan.

"Are you really not going to offer an old woman a seat and some refreshment?" she asked, feigning indignity.

Ivan and Cyras both extended apologies. While Cyras showed Aribella to a seat, Ivan took a straight line toward the bar.

"Sherry, if I remember correctly?" Ivan offered.

"Should I pretend to be surprised you remembered?" Aribella smiled back.

"Never," Ivan replied. "Let me see now," he muttered, picking up bottles and returning them to their places. "I don't see any sherry, but it appears someone had an affection for apricot brandy. Will that suffice?"

"It will have to," Aribella replied with a smile.

When Ivan handed her the glass, she took a tentative sip. "Not bad," she said and took a longer draft. "Now, I did some research into the girl's mother on my way here."

"Oh," Ivan and Cyras both exclaimed in unison.

She rolled her eyes at them and continued. "It seems Genevieve had an ancestor with elemental abilities. She was generations away from him and the line was absolutely polluted with humans. I don't know if there was enough genetic memory to be awakened by Alexia's father or not. It is, however remote, a possibility. I'll know more when I look at her."

Neither man spoke for a moment.

"Well?" she asked, looking between them.

"Do you know who Skeat's father is?" Ivan asked.

"That is a hideous nickname for a child. I prefer to use her proper name, thank you. Now, what were you saying about her father? Cyras said he's one of the turned. What else would be remarkable about him?" Aribella was beginning to suspect something was going on.

Ivan glanced at Cyras, who shook his head subtly. He had left out something significant.

"The girl's father is Alex, one of Grace's and Ben's sons," Ivan replied hesitantly.

Aribella's eyes went wide. She gasped and began giggling, unable to control herself for several moments, clasping her hand against her chest. One final deep breath, pushed out with deliberate force, seemed to calm her. Cyras and Ivan shared a look of concern as Aribella downed the rest of her brandy.

"Are you all right?" Ivan asked with concern.

"All right? I am more than all right. I am ecstatic. It's one thing to be called to read an ordinary human turned, but I never believed I would live to see a turned descendant of actual gods!" she exclaimed.

"We're not gods," Alex said, as he and Kitty entered the room.

"You may not think so, but to the inhabitants of this planet, you have always been seen as such. It's a matter of perspective, Aleksander Balderson," Aribella disagreed.

Alex stopped in his tracks, almost causing Kitty to run into his back. An icy shudder ran through him upon hearing a name no one had uttered since the fall of his world. The sound of it was foreign to him while simultaneously painful.

"I don't use those names anymore. My family uses Odinson as a surname, if you insist on one, but I prefer to be called Alex," he replied with an insincere smile.

Aribella hesitantly nodded at him. He may have been smiling, but the unmistakable warning that came from his eyes unnerved her in a peculiar way. The quiver of her bottom lip was nearly imperceptible to anyone, aside from him, as she spoke.

"Of course … Alex." Aribella's eyes flashed back to Ivan and her demeanor calmed. "I'm ready to see the child now."

As she rose from her seat, Alex moved between her and the stairs, bringing his hands up in front of him in a stopping motion.

"I'm sorry, who are you?" he asked, looking between Aribella, Cyras, and Ivan.

Ivan placed his hand on Alex's shoulder, pulling his attention away from the old woman. "Alex, this is Aribella Goodwind. She is a reader, and she is here at my invitation." He decided it best to leave out the part about her being with the Alliance.

Alex shrugged off Ivan's hand. "It looks like many people are here at your invitation. Why are you bringing more people here when we should leave?"

Ivan grasped Alex's shoulder with a firm hand and closed the distance between them. "We need to be able to tell Skeat what's going on. It may be detrimental to her if we rip her out of this place without being able to properly inform her of where we're going and why."

Under his words, Ivan was simultaneously speaking to Alex through a direct link. *I am very concerned about the damage she may cause to both worlds if we take her against her will.*

Alex backed up and nodded. "Whatever you feel is necessary, Ivan. I'm just concerned about the Alliance. We need to leave before they send someone to assess her."

"That's already been taken care of. We will have a reasonable amount of time to make sure she can be moved safely," Ivan replied, glancing at Aribella.

"Well, it seems settled then. May I see the child now?" Aribella asked, taking a step forward.

The men let her pass. As she grasped the railing, she looked up, hesitating before lifting her foot to the bottom step. As eager as she was to see the child, she was equally anxious at the amount of resistance her knees were about to provide for her. With an obvious effort, Aribella began her climb.

Three steps in and her legs had already begun their protest, crackling and quaking under her svelte weight. She plodded on, taking each step slower than the last.

"Would you like …" Ivan began to offer until an insulted glance from Aribella silenced him.

"I am perfectly capable of conquering a single flight of stairs, thank you," she said, stiffening her posture and raising her nose into the air.

Her genuine hope was whatever she was able to glean from this child would be worth the effort she was putting into this climb.

CHAPTER FOURTEEN

Aribella lingered in the doorway, observing the child before entering the room. Ignoring the girl, she quietly made her way to the window seat by the desk where the child sat. She relished the relief to her knees when the weight came off as she sank into the soft cushion of the alcove. She turned her head away from the child to admire the view from the window and began staring off into the distance. Aribella sat for only a few minutes when she began noticing the girl looking at her from her periphery. Aribella rubbed her thumb along a symbol on the staff, causing a faint pulsating glow to emanate from all the symbols.

The shine captured Skeat's attention. She cut her eyes to the side to examine the elderly woman who had invaded her space. The woman was simply sitting there, rubbing her thumb in a slow circle.

Aribella could tell the girl's curiosity was building. Her covert glances had become less subtle and longer lasting until she had fully turned in her seat to watch the staff breathing with light. Aribella maintained her outward gaze. It was a technique she had used often on frightened animals. Stay calm. Allow them to become comfortable with you invading their space until they have enough courage or curiosity to approach. It was a tried-and-true tactic that worked with animals and people alike as long as you had patience. And boy, did Aribella have patience.

Almost two full hours later, Aribella was, for the first time in her life, grateful for the callus that had plagued her thumb. If not for the toughness of it, the constant interaction with the raised symbol would undoubtedly have rubbed the skin raw.

Skeat had gradually crept across the room and was at present standing directly in front of her. Aribella felt the girl's eyes on her and casually rotated her head in the child's direction. Saying nothing, she smiled and ceased the circling motion of her thumb. The glow ebbed away, to Skeat's displeasure.

Skeat scrunched her nose and narrowed her eyes under a furrowed brow. It was an expression that Aribella could only decipher as a mixture of anger and pouting. The old woman slid her hand down the staff and pointed to a lower symbol across from Skeat's shoulder. The child's expression morphed to one of distrust. As Aribella swept her index finger across the symbol, a burst of colors erupted from the staff, creating a mesmerizing visual spectacle.

Skeat gasped and hopped backward. Aribella nodded to the girl to mirror her touch. Skeat stretched forward hesitantly, unwilling to lessen the distance her leap had given. She hastily poked the symbol, unsure if it would result in a shock of some sort. She giggled silently when the staff momentarily burst to life with a rainbow of color.

Taking an almost imperceptible step forward, Skeat once again reached out to touch the symbol, while Aribella watched attentively. It wasn't the symbol that was causing the staff to pulsate. Aribella made that happen. The display was purely to compel the child to contact the staff long enough for Aribella to get a read of her. Skeat slowly rubbed the symbol the way Aribella had. The rainbow of light slid from the staff along the walls and ceiling of the room, dancing at the speed at which the child brushed her finger over the spot. Soon the entire room was alive with swirling color.

Aribella had seen all she needed. She was still holding her staff in her right hand. Suddenly, she made a chopping motion on her right forearm with her left hand. She knew it wasn't totally correct, but she hadn't much choice with the position she was sitting in.

Skeat jumped back, enlarging her eyes to the size of saucers, ignoring the presentation of light slipping back toward the staff. Aribella leaned the staff against the wall and signed the words, "hello, my name is A-r-i-b-e-l-l-a. What is your name?"

Hot tears cascaded down the child's face, and her body trembled. How could this strange old woman know the secret language her momma had taught her? Emotion overwhelmed her and her skin flushed. She didn't know if she could trust this woman. What she did know was that she was grateful the world had finally brought her someone who could understand her. Skeat lifted her small hands with guarded optimism, convinced this wasn't real and the woman only wanted a laugh at her expense. She hastily signed back, "my name is L-e-x-a."

Once Aribella signed back, "It is nice to meet you Lexa," the child couldn't hold back any longer. Lexa launched herself forward, knocking Aribella backward into the wall with a force that was sure to cause her back to be sore for several days. The collision sent a shockwave through their bodies, but it was the child's desperate sobs, resonating in their embrace, that truly overwhelmed her.

~~~~

It had been half a day since Aribella had gone upstairs and Alex had grown anxious.

"What is taking so long?" he asked as a sour scowl covered his face.

"It will take as long as it needs taking," Ivan replied, looking up from what he was reading.

Alex flopped back against the cushion, reminding Kitty of an angsty teenager.

"Why don't you go for a run if you're so bored?" Kitty suggested from her meditative position on the floor across from Cyras.

"Because the minute I leave, they're going to come down and I'll miss the whole thing!" Alex complained. His lack of patience in this situation made him horrible at waiting.

"Why do you even care? You're going to abandon her anyway," Kitty stated in a relaxed tone, conflicting with the hostility of the message.

"You're such an asshole, Kitty. Why would you think I don't care? Because I think she deserves more than somebody like me?" Alex snarled back.

"No! Because you're not even bothered enough to try," Kitty argued.

"That's enough!" Cyras snapped. "Kitty, you don't get to judge another person's motives."

Alex mocked Kitty with a smug expression.
~~~~

"And you," Cyras turned to Alex, who promptly dropped the expression. "Try setting a better example than resorting to name calling. You're both acting childish."

The room fell silent as the dressing down was interrupted by the distinct clicking sound of the latch on Skeat's door, immediately followed by the unmistakable sound of the wooden slab sliding across the carpet. The four sprung to their feet, anticipating desperately sought answers.

Aribella grasped the railing at the top of the stairs in one hand, employing her staff to balance her descent in the other. Skeat trailed closely behind, gripping tightly onto Aribella's skirts as if the woman would cease existing if she wasn't touching her. The girl was not about to let anything separate her from the only person on the planet who could understand her.

Apart from the episode in which she was trapped in the bubble with the tanned, muscular man and the brief interaction with Aribella, she felt utterly abandoned. She wasn't exactly fearful of these people in her house, but she was concerned about why they were here. Two of the men were familiar from her cherished images and assuredly had been here in the past as she had witnessed with her own eyes. Eyes that were reflected back to her by the younger man's own. The quiet was what scared her. She could constantly hear her mamma and poppy's thoughts, but these people were silent aside from when they spoke with their mouths. As much as the overwhelming noise of the orphanage unsettled her, the quiet was more uncomfortable.

Lexa was a little overwhelmed with everyone staring at her as they descended the stairs. Her wide eyes met with Aribella's as the woman reached down and stroked the girl's hair as she smiled.

Turning back to Ivan, Aribella took a moment before she responded. "You may be surprised to know that her hearing is intact. She is also a telepathic receptor, but she doesn't know how to regulate it. It's like hearing through a radio that's always on and never properly adjusted to a single channel. Most telepaths are born closed and have to learn to push and pull to send and receive thoughts. She was born open and receives everything unless those around her are actively blocking, which is why she can't hear any of our thoughts, as blocking has become a habit for us. She doesn't respond to speech because she has difficulty distinguishing between real speech and private thoughts.

"What she's done is train herself not to respond to external stimulus, but in places like the orphanage there were too many. She was overwhelmed because she couldn't filter them or shut them out.

"As far as her speech is concerned, Ivan was pretty spot on. It seems like some links are fused together. She recognizes and understands communication, but she is unable to form the words to reply either telepathically or verbally. The girl signs like a daemon, though, and she's pretty funny, too." Aribella explained, flashing a quick, impish smile at the child.

"Daemon? Are you saying her mother was part daemon?" Alex asked, concerned.

"What? No. It's an expression," Kitty admonished. "Never mind. I got this."

Kitty stepped forward and knelt down in front of Skeat. She grappled to sign, "h-i S-k-e-a-t." Kitty knew little sign language, and she wasn't even sure this was the correct dialect, but with what she knew combined with using the girl's tablet, she was confident they could build an understandable form of communication.

"Hi!" Lexa signed back, grinning, and bouncing noticeably on her heels. She wasn't altogether certain if she liked the nickname Kitty had bestowed upon her. For the time being, she was willing to let it go because there were now two people she could talk to!

The chamber in her mind was dark and lonely, but a glimmer of hope shone through an ajar door, casting a narrow strip of light. As hard as her Poppy had tried before he passed, Lexa hadn't had any proper communication since her mother died. Prior to three months ago, she scarcely had any memory of being off this mountain, let alone being exposed to other people in the way she was at the orphanage facilities. The chaos she had experienced was much more than any nine-year-old should be expected to handle.

"Kitty?" Aribella asked.

"Yes?"

"She prefers to be called Lexa."

"Oh. Well then, Lexa it is." Kitty grinned while a pink blush spread over her cheeks.

"Can you fix it?" Alex asked, looking around the room, wondering why everyone was ignoring the obvious issue.

Kitty scoffed loudly at him. "IT? She's not broken, you asshole. There's nothing wrong with her."

Alex flushed hot with embarrassment as his eyes landed on Lexa, looking up at him with a mixture of anger and shame. He squirmed uncomfortably against the child's humiliated glare.

"That's not what I meant!" he snapped back at Kitty.

Ivan intervened, not thinking the child should be exposed to them fighting. He didn't believe Alex had meant any harm by what he remarked, but it had been insensitive.

"It should be simple enough to teach her how to block out the unwanted voices," Ivan said as he smiled down at the girl.

Lexa mustered a weary smile for him, nodding at the suggestion.

Instead of being grateful for the intercession, Alex only became angrier. "I don't need you to mitigate my intentions. I want to know if her speech can be fixed, so she doesn't have to suffer with this abnormality."

Cyras studied Ivan for a clue of what to do in this uncomfortable situation as the women let out a collective groan at the sheer indignity of what Alex had said.

Ivan took Lexa by the hand and led her out the front door.

"Where in all hells are you going?" Alex demanded.

Ivan didn't acknowledge his demand and as soon as he shut the door behind him, Kitty turned viciously on Alex.

"What the hell is wrong with you!? Why would you say something like that in front of her?"

Alex raised his voice to match hers. "What's wrong with *me*? What's wrong with all of you!? Do you not think she already knows she's different? Don't you think she deserves to be normal if she can be?"

"That's not the point, you *idiot!*" Kitty screamed back, stepping closer to Alex.

"What is the point exactly? To sugar coat everything? To make her think she's like everyone else? Because she's not. And dancing around it and coddling her feelings won't change that. She wasn't upset with the question until you pointed out that it was a horrible thing for me to ask."

"She's not a grown ass adult, moron! Lexa is a child with childish feelings and you crushed those feelings because you want her to be like you!" Kitty continued to yell.

"You crushed those feelings, not me. You were the one who made her feel like I was disgusted by her," Alex punctuated the thought by pointing accusingly at Kitty. "And you are sadly mistaken if you think I want her to be anything like me!" Alex took an aggressive step toward Kitty and pointed into his own chest. "What I want is for her to be able to talk to people."

"She may never be able to talk to people," Kitty sneered.

Suddenly, Aribella's staff cut between them with a force that sent both reeling several steps backward.

"That's enough," she said sternly, without raising her voice. "This is not solving anything. It doesn't matter at this point whether or not her communication issue can be resolved. What is important is learning how to communicate with her as she is now and teaching her how to block out the unwanted thoughts."

Alex ran his hand through his hair and took a step back. He began shaking his head as his body began to tremble. As the anger withdrew, overwhelming anxiety consuming his every thought replaced it. "I can't do this," he mumbled, casting his eyes toward the floor, and retreating another step. "I ... I can't do this," he repeated louder.

Kitty's eyes grew wide, knowing he was about to bolt. She took a step toward him, causing him to thrust his hands out in front of him and stumble backward toward the kitchen. "Alex?"

"No."

"Alex?" Kitty approached him slowly, holding her hand out to him. "We can figure this out."

Kitty had only taken two steps closer to him when he disappeared. He hadn't ported out; he had run. She could practically see the hot scent trail he had left in his wake. The French doors to the kitchen balcony bounced off the door stops with a dull thud and came to rest in a wide-open position. She ran to the railing and glimpsed thick foliage moving in a straight line away from the cabin.

"Fuck!" she yelled, jumping at the balcony railing aggressively. She threw her foot on top of the railing, fully intent on chasing him down.

Cyras reached her before she could jump and pulled her down by her shoulder. "Give him some time, Kitty. He'll be back," Cyras said to calm her aggression.

"He doesn't have time, Cyras! That kid needs him and all he can think about is himself!" Kitty spat back, jerking out of his grasp.

"Being angry with us will not make him come back any faster," Aribella admonished while moving through the doorway.

"I'm not angry! I'm disappointed in finding out how much of a coward he is!" She leaned over the railing, yelling at Alex's back.

"Well, it's us you're yelling at, dear," Aribella said and offered a supportive smile.

Kitty let out an exasperated huff before flopping into one of the lounge chairs around a small table. She looked back over the railing, watching the disturbance in the trees moving further away. She clenched her jaw at the sight as she let her anger seethe.

Cyras took a seat across the table from Kitty. "I can't blame him for walking away. Actually, I think it was quite the mature thing to do given his past."

"We all have pasts. That's no excuse for running away."

"It is a very mature thing to do when your past involves annihilating the populations of entire planets."

Kitty grunted at what she believed to be Cyras's extremely exaggerated recounting of made-up tales. "Mature? He ran like a coward."

Aribella leaned against the rail, interested in how this conversation was about to unfold.

"A coward, you say?" Cyras asked, showing an exuberant amount of concern by leaning forward and rubbing his chin.

"Yes!" Kitty declared emphatically. "He's running from his responsibilities to his own child. Her mother is dead, she needs him, and he ran!"

"All he did was ask a valid question, Kitty. It may not have been in the most appropriate way, but it was valid. You're the one who started an argument in front of the girl."

"Me?! You're blaming me for this?" She turned to Aribella for support. "Can you believe my own grandfather is trying to blame me for that man-child's behavior?" Kitty scoffed, crossed her arms, and slunk back in her chair like a teenager being scolded for staying out past curfew.

Cyras dropped his arm onto the table with his palm outstretched toward her. "Why are you being so adversarial toward him?"

"I'm not!" she exclaimed defensively.

Cyras cocked his head to the side, giving an accusatory stare.

Kitty dropped her eyes, squirming against the familiar look for several minutes. "He makes me angry," she mumbled.

"How is his asking if there is a way to help her make you angry? Isn't that something you would expect a father to ask?"

Kitty grabbed the edge of the table. "He doesn't care about her! He's planning on dumping her off with the first family that will take her off his hands!"

"Like I did when I let the pack raise you after your parents died?" Cyras hadn't said the words with malice, although they struck her just the same.

"No!" she exclaimed. "That was different. I knew you couldn't take care of me, but you were still there in all the ways that mattered."

"And what makes you think he won't do the same? You don't know anything about him. You don't know his situation and you certainly can't predict what he may or may not do. It seems you are condemning him for some image of the future you have in your head." His voice was calm and pointed as he tried to understand the situation. "So why are his actions making you so angry?"

Kitty leaned forward, increasing her grip on the edge of the table in front of her. "Because he's not giving her a choice!"

"A choice about what? She's nine. Lexa doesn't know anyone here except for you. She doesn't even understand what she is, much less the precarious situation that she's in. It's his responsibility to make the best choices for her, and he has decided taking her home is the best choice," Cyras explained.

"It's not her home!" Kitty asserted.

"That's not your business," Cyras replied dryly.

The statement enraged Kitty further, and she jerked herself up from her chair, stomped over to the railing and flung herself off without a sound except for the crumpling of leaves on which she landed. Cyras watched as she tore through the path Alex had taken. He was relieved that whatever confrontation was about to take place was going to happen away from the girl.

Aribella hobbled forward, taking the freshly vacated seat. Standing for such a long time had not done her knees any favors, and she groaned as she lowered herself. Cyras sighed and shook his head, watching the rustling trees become more distant.

"It could have been worse," Aribella said, resting her staff against the table.

"There's still time," Cyras quipped.

CHAPTER FIFTEEN

Kitty mumbled angrily to herself as she followed Alex's scent trail. Arguing with her wolf side was more like arguing with a different perspective of herself than it was speaking to another person altogether. She and her wolf were the same being, but didn't always see things the same way. It was kind of like a little voice in the back of her head that could answer her. Her wolf offered different opinions, but they weren't wholly separate personalities.

Why am I chasing after him? This is his family, not mine, her wolf side argued.

"Because somebody needs to talk some sense into him." Kitty grumbled aloud.

Ivan seems sensible. He doesn't seem at all upset about how Alex is reacting.

"Just because Ivan isn't acting upset doesn't mean he isn't."

That's a ridiculous argument. I don't know either of them well enough to know if this is normal behavior for Ivan or Alex.

"Well … Lexa needs someone stable in her life. Everyone has abandoned her."

Ivan seems like he's stable, and I don't think he came all this way to abandon her. Besides, everyone else in her life didn't abandon her. They died.

Kitty clenched her jaw. "This isn't about Ivan. It's about Alex taking responsibility."

There's no reason to think he won't, eventually. It sounds like he has a sizeable support system on Rasa and it's reasonable to think he's in shock about the whole situation. He's only known for a few days. He didn't even know she was a girl when he went to get her.

"I can't know that, can I?"

It doesn't matter. Cyras was right. It's none of our business. There are a lot of other kids out there who need help, and she isn't one of them. She's her family's responsibility now.

"That doesn't make me feel any better about leaving her with a father who resents her!"

Oh! So, it's all about you then, is it?

"No! None of this is about me."

Alex watched Kitty storm past him from his stony perch on the other side of the stream. He was on his back, well above her head and far enough away he couldn't make out specific words of her rant. Branches hung over the rock he was lying on, camouflaging him from her view. He didn't think she could see him, but hoped the wind wouldn't shift and carry his scent toward her. He wasn't ready to talk to anyone yet. She continued downstream and began pacing back and forth, circling the spot where he had traversed the creek. He hadn't crossed where he did to avoid anyone following him. He did so because he had forgotten where the precipice was and was forced to double back through the water.

Go away, he thought.

As the words crossed his mind, Kitty's head snapped in his direction. He laid his head back, looking up at the sky through the branches. Leaves rustled downstream but didn't move closer.

I should go back to the cabin and leave him alone.

"I need to know what he's going to do with Lexa."

Why do I need to know? He's leaving tomorrow or the next day. I'll never see either of them again.

Kitty realized her conversation was moving in the same circles as her feet. She sniffed at the air and spun around quickly.

"Damn it!"

No scent, no reason to stay. That's a sign, right?

"Shut up!"

Kitty ended her internal battle and traced her steps back to where she had lost Alex's trail. She scanned the woods on the other side of the stream for several minutes.

"Alex! I know you're over there!" she yelled.

The unmistakable sound of splashing followed her voice coming from the direction he had last seen her. He turned his eyes to see her moving in a straight line which would lead her away from his position. She was bluffing. He decided this was as good a place as any to face whatever judgement she had made on him. He knew she'd only get angrier if she had to continue searching.

"You're going the wrong way, Kitty," he shouted, sitting up.

She turned in his direction, scanning the area where his voice had come from.

"Up here," he said, waving at her.

"Why are you hiding out here?"

"I'm not hiding. I was thinking." Alex turned, letting his legs dangle over the ledge.

"Thinking about how you're going to take care of your daughter?" Kitty stopped below the outcropping and tilted her head up toward him.

"Don't start with me, Kitty."

"Somebody has to. She can't take care of herself, Alex." Kitty leapt up to the rock and sat beside him.

"You don't understand."

"I don't understand what? That I care more about her than you do?"

"Maybe you do. Maybe I'm just a horrible, self-centered person who doesn't give a crap about anyone else," he said, swinging his legs back and forth.

"If that was the case, you would have already left. You would have ported away from here instead of running into the woods," Kitty replied. Her anger was softening. She felt sorry for the position he was in, but she didn't pity him. He had created this situation himself, whether it was an accident or not.

Alex snorted and picked at a rough patch on the stone. "I had to get out of there. Nothing I say or do is right."

"No parent gets it right the first time. You can learn," Kitty said.

"It doesn't feel that way. I've been screwed up for a long time, and I don't know how to fix it. All I see is the worst outcome in every situation. I am poison for anyone who gets close to me, so I push everyone away. I'm negative and pessimistic, and I can't see any way to get past it on my own."

"You can get help. I'm sure you have a lot of people on Rasa who can help you. But that kid needs you right now. She doesn't have anybody."

Alex twisted his neck so he was facing Kitty. "I'm afraid I'm going to do something to mess her up. She'll be better off with Ivan or my father."

Kitty bit her lip. He wasn't the selfish asshole she thought he was. He was scared and desperately needed help. She closed her eyes and rubbed her head, wrestling with a thought that had invaded her mind.

"Well, you said you had Ivan, your father, and his mate, and your brothers. That seems like a lot of people to help you."

"We're all strangers to her, but that could make it a good opportunity to get her settled into a stable family where she could get to know all of us with no pressure. I could get her a private tutor and find someone to train her to use her abilities. I could even build a cabin just like the one we have here, so she'd have something familiar," Alex said.

Kitty thought it sounded like he was making plans to keep her, but maybe needed a little extra push.

"So, you expect this hypothetical family to move out of their home and live in a cabin you haven't built yet so they can take care of Lexa?"

"Now that you say it out loud, it sounds a little ridiculous," Alex said, as his posture deflated.

She could already tell she was going to regret what she was about to propose. She took a deep breath and pushed it out anxiously.

"Okay, how long will it take you to build the cabin? A couple of months?"

"Uh … no. A … a day or two, maybe?"

"Oh!" The answer was not what she expected. It had completely blown what she was planning to offer off the table. "That's pretty quick."

"If you say so," Alex said. He had forgotten how much slower things moved here.

"Well, how long will it take to place her with someone you trust?" Kitty asked.

Alex was becoming suspicious about her motives with all the questions she was asking. Half an hour ago, she had been screaming at him and now she was being too empathetic.

"Why are you asking?"

Kitty swallowed hard and shifted her body around to face him. She bit her lip again as Alex moved to look at her. She had another idea.

"Well, I have a solution … a temporary solution." Kitty hesitated. Alex cocked his head and pulled back a little.

"You don't have to decide right now," she added.

"What are you thinking?" Alex asked, rolling his eyes. He was certain whatever convoluted plan she had concocted was going to be anything but simple.

"What if I came back with you for a couple of months until Lexa gets settled? Just until she's comfortable with your family? That way, you could get used to each other without being on your own and she wouldn't have to be alone, with no one she knows. That would give you time to find the right place for her or maybe even figure out you can handle her yourself. I mean, not really by yourself; with your family's help," Kitty said quickly, bracing for his immediate rejection of the offer.

With his elbows resting on his knees, Alex fixed his gaze on the ground. It was a practical solution. It would most certainly be a comfort for Lexa to have someone she trusted around, and Kitty could supply some vital input on the kind of family that would be best for her. He could even build a replica cabin to give her a familiar space to live in while he tried to figure out how much responsibility he could handle regarding the girl.

On the other hand, would it be a sensible idea to take Kitty to Rasa? They could barely be in the same room for five minutes without fighting. Granted, every argument so far had been about her pushing a traditional fatherly role on him, which made no sense given the turned clans were very similar to her packs when raising the young. Traditional family roles weren't overly prevalent in either species. What kind of reaction could he expect if he couldn't meet her narrow expectations? Maybe that was exactly what she needed to see. Lexa wouldn't be neglected if he didn't personally raise her. He would still be involved in her life if he weren't her primary caregiver.

"Okay," Alex said, twisting his head up toward her.

"Okay?" Kitty asked, cocking her head and narrowing her eyes. He had agreed too easily. Where were the strings?

"But," Alex said, raising a finger.

There they are, Kitty thought.

"I'm paying you. You'll come to Rasa as Lexa's nanny for three months."

"Damn straight, you're paying me!" Kitty replied, giving Alex a shove.

"And no fighting in front of her," Alex added.

"Agreed," Kitty replied, extending her hand.

Alex shook her hand, and with that, a deal with the devil was struck. The question was, which one was the devil?

CHAPTER SIXTEEN

Ivan stood with Lexa outside near the garage where Aribella's shuttle had settled next to Alex's. He leaned against it, watching as the curious child examined the exterior. She rubbed her hands over the smooth finish, which had cooled from the mountain breeze.

"I'm sorry if anyone made you feel like you're not exactly the way you should be. There's nothing wrong with you simply because you communicate differently."

Lexa shrugged without taking her gaze away from the object a few inches in front of her face.

Ivan felt a wave of melancholy emanate from the girl. He had no idea how much she understood about what was going on around her. Her world had fallen out from under her and there were many more difficult changes coming. He needed to figure out a way to understand her. Unlike other languages, signing had a physical component and would take effort for him to learn properly. A thought flashed through his mind. His face contorted into a skeptical appearance as he pulled his TAC from his pocket.

He opened it, drawing Lexa's attention as he pulled at the corners of the virtual screen to approximate the size of a sheet of letter paper.

"Lexa, can you come here, please?"

Lexa moved a few steps toward him, drawn by curiosity more than his request.

"Can you read?"

The girl tipped her chin down and back up in a small affirming motion.

"I'm going to say some words and I want you to sign them. The screen will display the sign with the words underneath. I need you to tell me if it is correct. Okay?"

Lexa nodded her head in agreement.

"Before we start, show me the sign for no."

Lexa held up two fingers.

"Is that 'no', or are there two signs for 'no'?" The moment the words left his mouth, he understood that her blank stare was a clear indication she couldn't respond to a compound question.

Ivan tried again. "Are there two signs for 'no'?"

Lexa nodded to answer. She held up one finger before she shook her head from side to side. She then held up two fingers before showing him a second sign using her closed fist, also moving in a sideways motion.

"Okay. If the sign on the screen doesn't match what Sadie says, tell me by signing no."

The girl took a quick scan around, looking for this Sadie person and assumed she must be connected through the device Ivan was using. She made a quick nod, agreeing to the rules of this game.

A short while into Ivan's education, they had repositioned to the front porch swing. Cyras and Aribella had joined them, bringing drinks and a large tray filled with both sweet and savory snacks. Ivan had looped his TAC to a sturdy silver chain provided by Aribella and placed it around Lexa's neck so Sadie could give voice to the signs she was using. Sadie had found the girl's signs to be a close enough match to Earth's Universal Sign Language—USL, that the enhanced AI was only making small mistakes in local dialect and translation into grammatically correct sentences for English.

"We need to develop a signal so Sadie will know when you are telling her the interpretation is wrong and that you're not just trying to say 'no'," Aribella said.

Lexa nodded. She and Aribella went through a slew of symbols that weren't signs, laughing at Sadie's interpretation of each, before landing on one that Lexa liked.

Ivan was fumbling through rudimentary signs, seeming to master only the very basics while Aribella and Lexa tried not to snicker too often. Cyras hadn't even attempted to sign. He felt the girl already had the best solution with the device around her neck. He would only be around for a little longer and believed trying to learn a new language at his age was a futile task.

"Ivan, can the device use a different voice?" Aribella asked.

Lexa cocked her head toward Ivan, awaiting an answer. She didn't know how a voice of her own should sound.

"Huh. I guess we should ask her," Ivan replied. "Sadie, can you approximate an age-appropriate voice when you are speaking for Lexa?"

"Approximating parameters," Sadie replied, and scanned Lexa for size, gender, and age.

"Would this be an appropriate auditory representation?" Sadie replied with a young female voice.

Lexa sucked in air quickly upon hearing it. Her eyes bounced back and forth, looking at nothing, before a small smile appeared on her face. She looked up at Ivan, as her smile grew into a wide grin, while she nodded.

"Yes, Sadie. That is an acceptable voice for Lexa," Ivan said.

Instantaneously, the child had the voice she had struggled to bring forth for as long as she could remember.

They continued for a few more hours until the sun began to fade. Aribella looked between Ivan and Lexa, satisfied with the bond that had begun to form.

"Lexa," she said.

The girl turned toward Aribella.

"It was lovely to meet you, dear, but I'm afraid it's time for me to leave."

Lexa sunk in her seat. "Do you have to?" the synthetic, childlike voice asked, as Lexa signed.

"I do," Aribella answered. "I'd be very pleased if you could stay in touch, though."

Aribella leaned in close as Lexa looked up at her.

"You would?"

"I very much would. I have given Ivan my contact details. You may write to me as often as you want, and I promise I will always reply."

Lexa glanced at Ivan before standing. She leaned forward, hugging Aribella gently, then backed up and signed, "thank you." If it hadn't been for the old woman, Lexa would still be unable to communicate with any of them, and she was grateful.

Both men stood as Aribella rose from her seat to the accompaniment of her joints creaking and popping in protest. They stood on the porch and watched her make her way to the shuttle. Lexa waved one last time, her hand lingering in the air as the vehicle lifted from the ground and vanished down the driveway with a low humming sound.

A pair of footfalls, crunching leaves, and displaced gravel caused Ivan to turn his attention to the right as two figures emerged from the side of the house. Alex had his device open in front of them as he and Kitty were discussing changing the office into a bedroom suite.

"Has the plan changed?" Ivan asked.

"Oh, hey Ivan." Alex looked over the top of the device display. "Um … no. This is for something else," he said, moving his attention to Lexa. He made a few gestures on his device and closed it.

"Kitty and I have been discussing what needs to happen and I think we've come up with something that will make Lexa's transition a little easier."

Kitty nudged him with her elbow.

He nodded at her. "But first I owe someone an apology." Alex took a few steps toward Lexa and knelt in front of her. "Lexa, I'm sorry if what I said upset you. I wasn't trying to be mean. I only wanted to help."

Lexa pursed her lips together and wrinkled her forehead. She signed to the accompaniment of Sadie's childlike voice emanating from the TAC around her neck. "Are you my father?"

It was a question she had been wanting to ask since she had first seen him. He looked like the man in the pictures her mamma had shown her.

Alex was knocked off balance by the bluntness of the question as well as the voice Sadie had given the child. He nodded slowly and replied, "I am."

"Are you going to send me back to the bad place?" she asked.

"No. I would never take you back there." Alex replied. The hurt was profound as he grappled with the realization that she thought him capable of something like that.

"Are you going to go away and leave me here?"

"I'm going to take you back to where I live," he answered. The thought that she had overheard the many times he said he didn't want her made him ill.

"But what if my poppy comes back and I'm not here?"

His stomach sank, and he looked up at Ivan for a sign of what he should do. How was he supposed to handle that kind of question? Fortunately, Kitty stepped in to save him.

"Lexa, I'm sorry, but your poppy isn't coming back. He died," Kitty said, kneeling down beside Alex.

The girl's chin quivered as she cast her eyes down to the ground. "Like momma?" she asked.

Kitty felt so horrible for Lexa. In that moment, she realized every time she chased the child down, Lexa was trying to get back home to the only family she thought she had left.

"Yes, Lexa. Like your momma," she said, in a low voice that carried a soft, sympathetic tone.

She reached forward to place her hand on Lexa's arm, but the child rolled her shoulder and adjusted her body to the side. Her eyes remained cast toward the gravel. She sniffed and wiped her cheeks with the back of her sleeve. When she looked up, her eyes were rimmed with red, making her deep green orbs even more prominent.

"What if your other family doesn't like me?" Lexa signed, peering up at Alex sadly, biting her lip.

"I don't have another family. The image you have is my brother and his family. I have two brothers who look exactly like me," he said.

Alex could tell she didn't believe him by her frown and wrinkled forehead.

Kitty rose up and repositioned herself to stand between Ivan and Cyras.

"He's on his own for this one," she whispered to the men.

Alex pulled up a photo on his TAC and showed her.

"This is me," he said, pointing to himself on the left. "And this is Erik in the middle, and Mikkel on the right. They're your uncles. And you have some cousins and an aunt, but she's younger than you, so you have to be careful when you meet her."

"Are they all quiet too?" Lexa asked.

"All except for Una, your aunt. She's only two, so she hasn't learned how to be quiet yet."

"Do you think they will like me?" Lexa's demeanor hadn't changed. When not speaking, she displayed her hesitation and nervousness by tightly intertwining her fingers until her knuckles turned white.

"I do." He leaned forward and gave her a warm smile. "Who wouldn't like you?"

Lexa's body shrunk back, and she anxiously chewed her bottom lip and raised her sad eyes to Alex's.

"Lexa, do you think I don't like you?" Alex asked.

She nodded slowly.

He felt a wave of devastation overcome him at her simple gesture. As he looked at the tiny, frightened girl, he couldn't help but feel her pain of being unwanted and abandoned, surpassing any pain he had ever experienced. His greatest fear had come true. He had caused her suffering. Was this the sensation people described when they talked about love? How could this elusive idea, which everyone sought so fervently, be so heartlessly cruel? His urge to flee from the situation nearly consumed him, but he remained rooted in place, unable to move with her standing in front of him, looking up at him like that. What he wished most was to take away her sorrow.

He wanted to reach out and hold her, to offer her comfort and assurance that she was not alone. He had to be there for her, to support her, and to show her she was worthy of love and belonging. Overwhelmed by a sense of helplessness, he knelt there, uncertain of how to repair the damage.

With a trembling hand, he reached out and gently touched her shoulder, offering a small gesture of reassurance. His touch conveyed a silent promise—that he would be there to protect and care for her, no matter what.

"I was afraid you didn't like me," he said.

"If you liked me, why did you leave us?" she asked, shifting her gaze downward.

It was another unexpected question. Being honest with her was crucial for both of them.

"I didn't mean to. Your momma never told me about you." He hadn't meant to blame Gen, but the words had come out before he figured out another way to say it.

Lexa pressed her lips together and nodded, taking a step back. Alex wasn't sure what the nod was meant to convey as he dropped his hand back to his side.

"Can I bring anything with me?" she asked.

He hadn't thought about the girl's possessions. How much could a little girl have, anyway?

"Why don't you pack up your most favorite, special things? Would those all fit into one or two bags?"

Lexa nodded again, but more slowly this time, like she was thinking about what she could take. Then she turned and walked away from him into the house.

CHAPTER SEVENTEEN

Alex woke up early the next morning. The two things on his agenda were to start closing up the house and make a brief visit to Vito. He knew he owed Vito an apology. It would still be early afternoon in Italy, so he thought it best to get that out of the way first. When he opened his door, he could see that Lexa's door was ajar, giving him a glimpse of her empty bed. She had gone to sleep early the night before, having skipped dinner, and he figured she had slept long enough to have been up. He thought she might be in the kitchen and made his way down for a cup of coffee before he left.

The lights were off. Kitty was sleeping on the couch, even though Cyras had already left and there was an empty bedroom upstairs. Lexa wasn't there. He grabbed a cup of coffee and took a quick look around the downstairs rooms, to no avail. Had her pillows and comforter been hiding her in the bed? He wondered, as he climbed the stairs. Once at the top, he pushed the door in to see the window on the other side of her desk wide open, with the curtains hanging out.

Panic swept over him, and he quickly made his way over to the window. He caught her scent over the sill and down onto the front porch's roof. He set his cup down on the padded alcove seat and jumped out the window without thinking it through.

"Augh!" he yelled out, as a sharp piece of gravel cut a deep gash into the heel of his bare foot.

He bent back, balancing on the ball of his foot, and pulled out the jagged rock, allowing his blood to spill out over the ground. He stood and spun around until he had caught her scent again. Following the trail, he made his way to the dirt road behind the garage, which led to the old caretaker's cottage. The cold compacted dirt was soothing to his aching heel, but did nothing to quell his heart pounding loudly in his ears.

The once well-trodden narrow road had become a forgotten route, swallowed up by the encroaching vegetation. Sprinting as fast as he could, Alex covered the half mile to the cottage in mere seconds. When the path opened into a clearing, the old cottage stood in ruins in front of him. The bare skin on his arms, legs, and face were covered in quickly healing scratches which left trails of wet, sticky blood all over him. He turned right, then left, picking up Lexa's route down a narrow path leading deeper into the woods. Approaching the trail, he could feel her close by, and was overwhelmed with relief. He cautiously walked through Lexa's freshly pressed path, wiping blood off with his black shirt as he went. His coming out of the woods in the dark, covered in blood, was the last thing he wanted her to see.

When he stepped out from the last turn, the moonlight illuminated two headstones. Lexa sat between them, taking a single flower from the pile on her lap, and placing it on one of the two graves, then repeating the action for the other.

Alex stepped closer. "Lexa, what are you doing?"

Lexa didn't raise her head, nor stop her flower bestowment ceremony. "Saying goodbye to momma and poppy." She paused her ritual long enough to sign then continued her rhythm.

He walked closer, peering into the woods beyond at no fewer than fifty grave markers of past caretakers, all belonging to the same lineage. It was a somber reminder there was no one left to care for the property once they were gone. Lexa was the last of her human line. Maybe they should turn it over to Vito, or possibly Kitty would want it when she was finished with her job on Rasa. But it wasn't his to give. It was Ivan's.

Alex sat in front of her and watched. The cold, dampness of the ground quickly seeped through the thin material of his shorts, sending a chill shuddering through him. The sweet scent of the mixed bouquet carried toward him and mixed with the mounded dirt from Mato's grave. Gen's had long ago been covered by forest moss. The care the child took placing each flower into heart shaped patterns showed how deeply she had cared for her family. She needed family. She deserved family, not unrelated strangers. He shivered with both cold and apprehension while he waited for her to finish.

Alex was unsure how she was going to react when they took her away from here. He swallowed hard thinking over the right way to start the conversation they needed to have.

"Would you like it if Kitty could come for a little while until you get used to us?"

She nodded her head yes and fidgeted with the flowers, adjusting them into a larger shape.

He couldn't blame her for being nervous. He was nervous too.

"Are you sad that you won't be able to come back and see them again?"

Lexa shrugged, unable to look at him, and poked another stem into alignment.

"Would you like to come back and visit sometimes?"

She looked up at Alex and nodded timidly.

"We can do that."

"Really?" she asked.

"We live pretty far away, but I'll make sure we come back on your momma's birthday. Is that okay?"

"Promise?"

"Promise."

Lexa stood up so Alex did the same. She hugged each grave marker, then turned to face him.

"Are you ready to go back?"

Lexa nodded and Alex turned to walk back up to the cabin, when the girl surprised him by sliding her freezing cold hand into his.

When they got back, Kitty was in the kitchen. She stepped around the counter and gave Alex a side eye.

"Don't ask," he said, addressing his lack of attire fit for the weather. "Could you make her some breakfast? I have a few errands to run before we leave."

Lexa let go of Alex's hand and crossed the room to Kitty.

"Oh my god! You're freezing! We better start with some hot chocolate," Kitty said, rubbing Lexa's cold hands in her warm ones.

Alex went upstairs, changed, and ported out to atone for his accusations. He was back a few hours later, having been forgiven by Vito. This had been the longest week of his life. He had been on an unimaginable rollercoaster of highs and lows. He had lost his scruples, his reputation, and finally, hopefully, his paranoia would soon follow. But what he gained was something he never thought he wanted or needed.

By late afternoon, everything had been packed and covered. They were ready to go. Alex explained to Lexa that it would be morning where they were going but hadn't explained they would be going to another planet. He wasn't sure she would be able to comprehend it in the short time they had before they left. Kitty climbed into the back of the shuttle with the girl, both excited and anxious for different reasons. It was only after the shuttle lifted off that Ivan explained to the child that they would be going into space for just a few minutes before coming back down. Once they cleared Earth's atmosphere, and sensor range of the planet, Ivan shifted the shuttle into Rasa's orbit, and Alex began their descent.

Lexa pressed her face against the glass. When she had been in shuttles before, mostly with Kitty, they stayed low to the ground, following traffic patterns. This was the first time she had been high enough to see an entire city. It was bright and clean; unlike any she had seen before. They passed over, moving toward a mountain range beyond.

"Lexa," Alex said.

She pulled her face away from the window and leaned up between the front seats. The shuttle descended over a mountain road.

"I have a surprise for you."

"For me?"

"Yup. Keep looking out the front."

The shuttle descended below the tree line following a narrow dirt trail which opened up the higher they got. At the top of the road, in a large clearing, sat the cabin.

Lexa sucked in a quick breath. "How did my house get here?"

"It isn't exactly the same, but it's as close as I could get it," Alex said, while he landed the vehicle.

Lexa jumped out of the shuttle and ran up onto the porch, smelling and rubbing her fingers over the freshly built columns and railings. She jumped on the rigid floor, which refused to creak under her weight. With a broad grin, she leapt up to touch the brackets where the new porch swing would hang.

"Careful!" Alex yelled, as a swarm of construction drones buzzed around her, placing finishing touches on the exterior.

She followed them excitedly, hopping over the railing to trail them around the side of the house. As she disappeared from view, Kitty chased after her, taking in the clean scents and bright colors of the new planet.

Vivienne ported in on the temporary construction platform behind Alex and Ivan, followed by two service units carrying an immersion pod.

"What is that?" he asked.

"Nice to see you too," Vivienne replied, as Ivan lowered his head and smiled.

"Sorry, Viv. I wasn't expecting anyone to be up here."

"I won't stay long, and I've told everyone to let you get settled before they come visit. I just wanted to drop this off for you," she said, pointing to the pod.

"Well, what is it? I've already got a sleep pod."

"This is no sleep pod. It's a therapy pod," she said, unable to resist smirking at him.

"I don't need a therapy pod," he replied.

"You have a daughter and a woman you've only known for less than a week living with you. If anyone needs a therapy pod, it's definitely you."

Alex looked down, prodding the freshly laid gravel with his foot. "Thank you, Viv," he said.

After the pod had been installed, Vivienne and Ivan left. Alex stood in the driveway, staring up at the newly constructed version of the place that held happy memories, and watched as Lexa gleefully chased drones, and Kitty chased her. He resolved to use Vivienne's gift often over the next few decades to help him navigate the ups and downs of his new responsibilities. He wanted this cabin to become the center of many family gatherings, resolvable arguments and even a bit of drama, to keep things interesting.

He had no illusions his and Lexa's relationship would be without its struggles but hoped it would eventually grow into something they both valued. This was his chance for a fresh start; a reboot of sorts, where he didn't need to cling to his old fears. He was a different man than he had been last week. He hoped, a better man.

ALSO BY

JOYCE SERRANO

THE TURNED GODS SERIES

Original Grace - Book 1
Immortals in the Everything - Book 2
Gateway to The Nothing - Book 3

THE TURNED GODS - CHARACTER COMPANION SERIES

Galin's Alley
Lilly's Game
Alex's Claim